THE
MASK OF
AKHNATEN

By ROBERT SILVERBERG

THE MACMILLAN COMPANY
NEW YORK

Library of Congress catalog card number: 65–13586

The Macmillan Company, New York
Collier-Macmillan Canada, Ltd., Toronto, Ontario

Designed by Alan Benjamin

Map by Harry Rosenbaum

Printed in the United States of America

First Printing

CONTENTS

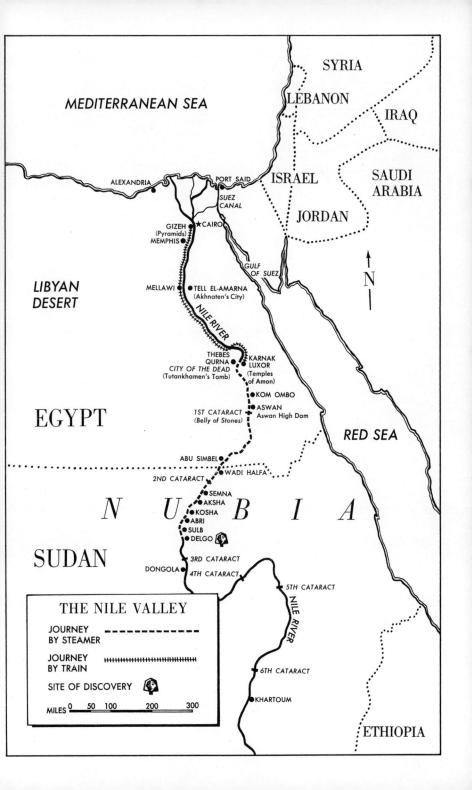

CHAPTER ONE

THE TOWERS OF CAIRO

The water was rising. A world was drowning, a world half as old as time. A huge dam, the newest of the monuments of Egypt, had risen to throttle the Nile, and moment by moment, as the penned-up water mounted, the relics of the past were being swallowed up.

But the dam and the drowning world were far to the south. As he stood by the window of his hotel room in Cairo, looking out at the broad sweep of the Nile, it was hard for Tom Lloyd to imagine the bleak desert world of Nubia. Nubia, and the drowning land, were what he had come to Egypt to see. But Cairo was a vast bustling city. It did not seem at all suited to his idea of what Egypt should be like.

Tom shaded his eyes with his hand against the blinding afternoon sunlight and stared at the city. He wondered how he was going to enjoy being exposed to that strong sun. His skin was tanned already, had been so since late spring. But the Egyptian sun was something extraordinary—it was a terrifying ball of fire blazing against the blue shield of a cloudless sky. Tom, a stocky dark-haired boy who was going to be fifteen in a month, didn't want to spoil his trip to Egypt with a severe case of sunburn.

1

Tom and his uncle, Dave Lloyd, had been in Egypt only a few hours. A soaring jet liner had carried them eastward in two big hops: New York to London, then—after a chance to stretch legs and a change of planes—onward to Cairo. Tom hadn't seen much yet. He and his uncle had stepped out of the plane into the shiny airport buildings, had gone through the red tape of international customs, and then they had boarded the bus for the hotel. Except for a dazzling glimpse of the pyramids as the jet swung round Cairo to make its landing approach, Tom hadn't seen anything of ancient Egypt yet.

But there was plenty of time. He had all summer ahead. Soon enough, Tom would leave Cairo. He and his uncle would trek southward into Nubia, into the area soon to be covered by the waters of the big lake created by the new dam. They were going to spend the summer watching archaeologists at work salvaging the treasures of the past before they would be engulfed forever.

The door of the hotel room opened, and Tom's uncle came in. He had gone down to the lobby to cash some traveler's checks. As he entered, he flourished a thick roll of colorful bank notes.

"Tom, we're rich men!" he exclaimed. "Look at these! The gold of the pharaohs!"

Tom took one of the bank notes. "Looks more like paper to me, Dave."

Dave Lloyd shrugged. "That's the whole trouble with the modern world," he said, in a mock-serious tone. "You can't jingle a sack of gold pieces at your hip any more. You carry a bunch of gaudy pieces of paper around instead. Here, have some. But remember, this stuff is real money—even without George Washington on it."

He counted out some of the Egyptian pound notes, which Tom knew were worth about a dollar and a half apiece, and some bills of smaller denominations. Tom folded them carefully and tucked them into his wallet. "Thanks, Dave."

His uncle nodded and walked past him, to the window. Tom had never wanted to use the formality of "*Uncle* Dave" when talking to Dave Lloyd, nor was it expected of him. In many ways, Dave seemed more like an older brother than an uncle. People often mistook the two for brothers. Dave was taller, not quite so wide across the shoulders. But uncle and nephew had the same unruly black hair, the same dark, inquisitive eyes, the same ready smiles. Dave Lloyd was the youngest brother of Tom's father. He was a little past thirty, and there were times when, to Tom, he seemed a lot younger than that.

The Nubian expedition had been Dave's idea. He was a writer, and a magazine had sent him on assignment to Nubia, to do a series of articles on the gigantic new dam being built and its effects on ancient archaeological sites. He was planning to turn his articles into a book about Nubia later. One night when Dave was visiting Tom and his family, Tom had said, "I wish I could go to Egypt some day."

"Why don't you come along with me?" Dave shot right back at him, and that was when the trip began.

It meant that Tom would have to give up summer camp, but that was no true sacrifice when measured against a trip to Egypt. It also meant drawing the money out of the bank account he had built so carefully. Tom had set up a little

3

fund for himself, out of his allowance and his vacation-job earnings. He hoped that by the time he was old enough to go away to college, there would be enough money in his account so that he could buy a car. But college was still three years in his future. And was a car really so important? he asked himself. His savings had finally gone toward the cost of his air fare. He figured that his summer in Egypt would be a good investment for the future, that it would give him a deeper understanding of the ancient past, that it would help him to see history as something more than words on a school-book page.

Actually, Tom and Dave Lloyd were not going to spend much of the summer in Egypt. They would simply pass through the land of the pharaohs on their way southward to the doomed monuments. Their destination was the neighboring country of Sudan—but they would travel along the Nile from north to south to reach their goal.

The Nile itself was directly outside their window. Tom joined his uncle and looked at it again. The wide river, a muddy blue, crept past slowly. A steady stream of freight vessels moved by in stately procession, carrying building materials and merchandise. Most of the freighters were flat wooden barges, curved upward at the prows. They moved along under patched and tattered sails. A low-slung highway bridge spanned the Nile near the hotel, and Tom watched as boat after boat lowered its sails and took down its bamboo masts to pass under the bridge.

"They haven't changed the design of those boats in four thousand years," Dave said. "They were good for hauling freight when the pyramids were being built, and they still come in handy."

4

"But Cairo itself has changed," Tom said.

"Cairo wasn't even here when Egypt was great. Cairo was built by the Arabs about a thousand years ago after they conquered Egypt because they needed a new capital. They called it '*El Qahira*'—'the Victorious.' The Egyptians found it easier to pronounce the name *Cairo*."

"A thousand years is pretty old for a city, though."

Dave Lloyd smiled. "Not here, Tom. Cairo was founded only yesterday. Out there, by the desert—where the pyramids are—that's old. Four, five times as old as Cairo. In Egypt, a thousand years goes by like the wink of an eye."

Dave turned away from the window. Tom remained a moment longer, looking at the sprawling city reaching toward the horizon. Cairo struck him as a city of towers. Here and there, like swords stabbing at the sky, rose the lacy towers of the Moslem mosques with their elaborate traceries of design. But there were other towers, too; a kind more familiar to Tom—skyscrapers, huge office buildings, hotels, apartment houses—shooting up out of the buildings clustered at their bases. Most of the skyscrapers were white and gleamed blindingly in the sun.

Automobiles crept at snail's pace through the narrow streets, their honking horns creating a symphony of discords. Tom could imagine the sweating drivers scowling in their cars as the traffic crawled along. Most of the cars were small and European-made, but the traffic jam itself was an American-looking sight. Through the snarl, there clattered an occasional horse-drawn cart, and Tom gasped with delight at the sight of a heavily laden camel being led down the street.

The contrasts were striking: the broad slow-moving Nile with its timeless wide-sailed boats, and the traffic-choked

5

street with its horde of noisy little cars. Camel and horse-cart seemed wildly out of place against the background of sky-scrapers. The fast-moving men in business suits who scurried along the sidewalks, brief cases flashing importantly, might have been plucked up from New York or Chicago and set down here. Among them sauntered Bedouins in desert costume, burnooses drawn over their heads, and Egyptians wearing the long white cotton robe called the *galabia*, half-opened to display waistcoats of bright colors.

Tom shook his head and stepped back from the window. It was all too confusing, too hectic to take in at a glance. His head was whirling. After so many hours aboard planes, he felt dizzy and exhausted.

Dave said, "We'll have an early meal in the hotel dining room and get to bed right afterward. That way, we'll get into the swing of things tomorrow. If we try to do any sight-seeing today, we'll never get adjusted to the local time zone."

"I agree. What time is it?"

"Four in the afternoon—Cairo time."

"And back home?"

Dave grinned. "Who knows? Who cares? We're in Egypt now—remember!"

Looking around the hotel room itself, Tom found that a bit hard to believe. It was a thoroughly American-looking room, complete with air conditioner. It was rather a disappointment. He had hoped for a more exotic lodging. But they would only be staying here a short while. Then they'd be heading down the Nile toward the monuments of Nubia.

No, Tom thought. Not *down* the Nile. *Up* the Nile. He had been making that mistake all the time. The Nile, unlike most rivers, flowed from south to north. When you went south from Cairo, you were going up the Nile. Cairo was in the northern part of Egypt, but that region was Lower Egypt. Upper Egypt was hundreds of miles to the south. Tom was used to thinking of the north as being "above" the south, as it usually looked on maps. But, in Egypt, all directions related to the flow of the great river.

Tom and Dave freshened up and left the room. A sleek, high-speed elevator zoomed them down and into the huge, lofty lobby. Murals done in ancient Egyptian style covered the walls. Here, a gigantic pharaoh smiled coldly out at a view of the pyramids. There, a crouching sphinx seemed about to spring at them. On another wall, prancing horses drew the chariot of a noble Egyptian lady who was shown in profile with ruddy skin and large dark tranquil eye.

There was noise in the lobby—a raucous hubbub.

"Look who's here," Dave said sourly. "Our friends from the plane!"

"I thought they were staying at a different hotel."

"I guess they've decided to keep us company. Well, let's be friendly, eh? They aren't bad sorts. Just a little on the noisy side."

Out of London, Tom and Dave Lloyd had shared the plane with a mob of tourists bound, like themselves, for Egypt. Although Tom was a tourist himself, he couldn't help wanting to stay aloof from these people. About twenty of them from various European countries were traveling together on a predesigned tour. During the entire flight, they had asked the silliest questions imaginable—always at the tops of their lungs.

Now here they were again, milling about the lobby—the

men wearing flamboyant sports shirts; the women, light frilly dresses. Everyone carried a camera. Some of them were holding thick stacks of guidebooks to Egypt—books that they probably hadn't read. Tom was amused by the sight. He hoped he wouldn't grow up to be like these loud, foolish people who were traveling through one of the world's most interesting places without really learning a thing.

There was one member of the group, though, who didn't seem stupid. He was the guide, the man in charge. Tom had watched him in action aboard the plane. He was a young man, perhaps about twenty-seven, very lean and wiry, with bushy black eyebrows, thin lips, and cheekbones that jutted out like the blades of a knife. His name, Tom had gathered, was Paul Kurtz. He spoke English perfectly, but with a trace of an odd accent. And he seemed to regard the tourists in his care as so many silly geese who had to be watched closely lest they get into trouble.

Tom hadn't liked him much. Kurtz had seemed sarcastic and curt. But he was obviously very efficient. And he seemed to know a great deal about Egypt.

The guide was over at the hotel desk now, probably making the arrangements for rooms for his people. Tom and Dave smiled at the group of tourists. A moment later, Paul Kurtz came striding across the lobby, his heels clicking with military precision against the marble floor.

"Everything is in order," he announced crisply. "We have accommodations in this hotel. The porters will take you to your rooms. You are to unpack and join me here in exactly one hour and thirty minutes."

Then he noticed Tom and Dave. He glanced at them, and a smile briefly crossed his bony face.

"So—we meet again," Paul Kurtz said.

Dave nodded. "I thought you and your people were staying on the other side of the city."

"There was a mistake in the reservations," Kurtz explained. His eyes gleamed with sudden hatred. Tom got the impression that Paul Kurtz would, if he could, cheerfully behead the clerk who had mixed up the reservations. "We found that our rooms were not available," Kurtz went on. "Luckily, we were able to obtain accommodations here."

"I thought Cairo's hotels were full this month," Tom said. "How did you get rooms?"

Kurtz's grin was chilling. "My organization has its influence. Certain other reservations were canceled to make room for us. That is all."

Tom frowned. "But that means that other people are going to show up and find that they don't have any rooms."

"And so? Was this not what happened to us?" Kurtz asked. "I must think of the comfort of my people here. I cannot worry about unknown tourists yet to arrive." Again he flashed his quick, unfriendly smile. "You will excuse me now. Perhaps we will see each other again as we travel through Egypt, yes?"

"I doubt it. Tom and I are heading pretty deep into Nubia."

The tourist guide studied them a moment without replying. Then he said, "We may still meet, then. I shall be going well into Nubia myself later this summer."

"Isn't that far off the usual tourist route?" Dave asked.

"The usual tourist routes are changing," Kurtz answered. "There are many who wish to see the Nubian monuments before the water covers them. I hope you enjoy your stay."

He pulled his heels together and nodded at them in his military way. Then he spun round and went off stiffly to tend to the needs of his noisy flock.

Tom shuddered. "I don't like him. Not one bit."

"He's harmless," Dave said. "He can't help being so formal and distant. I suppose you get that way if you spend as much time as he does with people like those."

Tom shook his head. "I got the feeling that he was laughing at us all the time he was talking to us. I don't know why. What he said *sounded* polite. But the look in his eyes—the tone of his voice——"

Dave laughed. "You shouldn't judge people on such short acquaintance, Tom. It's a poor habit. He's probably a studious young fellow earning a living as a guide, nothing more sinister than that. Maybe he's putting himself through some university by taking this job in the summer. And, probably, he doesn't realize that he rubs people the wrong way."

"But he said he simply forced a lot of people out of their hotel reservations to make room for his tourists," Tom protested. "Was that right?"

"Be practical, Tom. Here Kurtz is in Cairo with a couple of dozen helpless people. Somebody has goofed up and his flock has nowhere to stay. So he pulls strings and finds them a lodging. It happens all the time. What's he supposed to do with them—put them up in tents on the desert?"

"It might do them some good," Tom said, chuckling. "Toughen them up a little. They're a pretty flabby bunch, aren't they?"

"Wait till the Egyptian sun gets at them. It'll melt that flab away." Dave gestured toward the hotel dining room. "It'll probably melt *us* too. How about dinner?"

"Good idea," Tom agreed.

But, he soon found, it wasn't a very good idea at all. The food in the hotel was excellent, but he had no appetite. His body's time schedule was awry since the jet had taken them eastward across zone after zone, and this wasn't his normal dinner hour. It seemed more like the middle of the night than late afternoon. His head ached and buzzed. Excitement made his body throb. His usually hearty appetite fled. His uncle, too, seemed to be having trouble finishing his food.

Tom was yawning by the time dessert arrived. His eyes felt raw and weary. Several times his head lolled forward in a quick doze, and he had to catch himself and fight his way back to wakefulness.

Yet, when they went upstairs after dinner, Tom found it strangely hard to fall asleep. He was tired now, but not sleepy. Images jostled each other in his brain: pyramids and temples, camels and horses, the wide river and the sun-baked desert. The towers of Cairo rising up above the sprawl of the city glittered in his mind's eye.

At last, sleep came. With it, came dreams. Tom was far underground somewhere, squinting by dim light at the statue of an Egyptian monarch of thousands of years ago. Slowly, he lifted his flashlight, let the rays play over the pharaoh's face—and the face, he saw, was that of the tourist guide Paul Kurtz, with somber eyes, bloodless lips, and savagely sharp cheekbones. Then the dream passed, and no others followed it. Tom slept, the air conditioner purred gently, and boats drifted north to Alexandria along the wide river Nile as slumbering Egypt moved toward morning.

11

CHAPTER TWO

CAMELS AND PYRAMIDS

Two days later, Tom was fully adjusted to Egyptian time.
But he hadn't yet adjusted to the excitement of Cairo, to its
Oriental splendor and busy pace.

He and Dave had toured the city thoroughly. The modern
section of Cairo with its broad tree-lined boulevards, its
apartment houses and shops and movie theaters, was only a
part of the city. Tom and Dave had had a good view of it
from the Citadel on the hill overlooking Cairo. The Citadel
was the work of Sultan Saladin, who had fought valiantly
against the Crusaders in the 12th century. Below its lofty
ramparts, there were two magnificent mosques; medieval
Cairo lay just beyond.

They went down into the old part of the city. Tom had
to keep reminding himself that what he was seeing was not
really old, as Egyptian cities went, that the last of the
pharaohs had been in his grave for fifteen centuries when
Cairo was founded in A.D. 969. Yet, here was a maze of
twisting streets—too narrow for automobiles. Donkeys and
camels provided transportation, but Tom and Dave went
on foot. It was like stepping into the Arabian Nights. Here
was a bazaar—where haggling merchants dealt in scents and

12

spices, fine silks and gleaming satins. Here were small shops —behind their bead-fronted doors craftsmen toiled in wood or leather or metal. Peddlers chanted huckstering cries in Arabic. Small boys slipped through the crowd, hands outstretched for alms. Fat shopkeepers sat by their goods, puffing on hookahs, drawing the tobacco smoke through water before it reached their lips.

Shouts and complaints echoed in the air. It was not necessary to know Arabic to guess what was being said. Here, a dark-faced old man with flowing white beard showered vivid curses on another old man who apparently owed him money; not far away, a plump mother shrilled at a mischievous-looking boy of about six; a carter boomed abuse at a stubborn camel who had stopped dead in his tracks to stare around as if he were a tourist himself.

The city was so full of life, it hummed so with activity, that Tom hardly noticed the heat. He was too busy sightseeing. But hot it certainly was—close to 100°, Tom guessed. It was a dry heat, though. This was a country where rain never fell, and there was little moisture in the air. The sky was so blue it hurt the eyes to look up into the brightness. And there was always the great swollen sun somewhere above, baking everything.

The third day they were in Cairo, Dave announced, "Today we see the Pyramids at Gizeh, like all proper tourists. And tomorrow we get moving southward."

"Can't we stay in Cairo a few more days?"

"We'll be back here again at the end of the summer, Tom. There's more to see in Egypt than Cairo. And people are waiting for me in Nubia."

Tom couldn't quarrel with that. This was Dave's trip, after all—not a sight-seeing jaunt for him, but business. He couldn't spend his days prowling through the bazaars of Cairo. The magazine which had sent him wanted articles about what was happening south of the Aswan High Dam. So, fascinating as Cairo was, Tom resigned himself to a quick departure.

Paul Kurtz and his tourist clan had already left. The cold-eyed guide had whisked his group off to see the pyramids the day after their arrival, and, by now, they were probably well up the Nile. But there were plenty of other tourists around. Again and again, Tom saw the same scene repeated: a tourist aiming his camera at an Egyptian whose response was either to snarl in anger or to thrust out a hand for money.

"Why do they keep taking pictures of the people?" Tom asked. "Don't they see that it annoys them?"

"That doesn't matter to them," Dave said. "All they want is something to show the folks back home. Something picturesque and colorful. It doesn't occur to them that the people here don't like being photographed."

"They'd feel awfully annoyed if some Egyptians came to their home towns and began sticking cameras in *their* faces," Tom said. "Dave, are we going to get to meet any of the people? I mean, to get to know them, to find out what they're like? I don't want to be just another sight-seer. I'd like to make some friends here. Or is that a pipe dream?"

"We'll be living in a Nubian village for a few weeks," Dave said. "We'll have plenty of time to meet the villagers. I hope we can get to know them. We'll see."

But, for a time, Tom and Dave were content simply to go through the standard sight-seeing routines. They left the hotel early in the day and drove across to the west bank of the Nile. Barren pink and gray stretches of the Libyan desert confronted them now, and, at the edge of the desert, stood the pyramids. They had their choice of transportation to the pyramids: car, camel, donkey, horse, or foot.

"Let's splurge and take a camel ride," Tom suggested.

Dave had no objections. The camel drivers spoke English since this was the first stop for most visitors to Egypt, and it was a simple matter to hire a couple of camels for the ride. Tom began to have second thoughts as he got close to his beast. The camel was tall, shambling, and astonishingly ugly, and it had a habit of rolling back its big lips to show a set of nasty teeth. Its owner uttered a sharp command; the camel lowered itself to the ground, knobby knees bending weirdly.

"You get on now," said the camel driver, grinning encouragingly.

Tom took a deep breath and clambered into the saddle. The strange beast immediately quivered and swayed and got to its feet, rear end first. Tom wasn't expecting things to happen quite that way, and he found himself being thrown forward violently. He grabbed for the edge of the saddle, expecting to go flying over the camel's head. Abruptly, all was still, and he was snugly seated.

Dave, too, was mounted. "How are you doing?" he asked.

"Fine—I think. I feel a little seasick."

"Wait till he starts to move!"

Tom made a wry face. "Whose idea was this, anyway?"

"Don't look at me," Dave said.

The camel driver caught the reins of Tom's mount and tugged. The camel went into motion and they started toward the desert. Riding was a curious, but not altogether unpleasant, sensation. The camel lurched along, swinging and jouncing. There didn't seem to be much relation between what the front legs were doing and what the back legs were doing at any given time. But, after a few moments, Tom got used to the odd, jerky rhythm of the ride and actually began to enjoy it.

Tom was so busy concentrating on his camel ride that he failed to notice the pyramids when they first came into view. Dave had to tell him to look up.

There they stood! Forty-five centuries had passed since the youngest of them had risen. A tingle of awe ran down Tom's spine. They were not really attractive, these three colossal piles of rough stone. They rose out of a backdrop of light brown sand which was broken in places by tufts of scrubby grass. The stones were weather-beaten and worn, and the stark majesty of the sight was lessened by the presence of a horde of camera-clicking visitors.

But not even the eager photographers could effectively mar the grandeur of the pyramids, Tom thought. Vast and mysterious, titans out of a remote past, they numbed the eye with their size and strangeness. The tourists who clustered around them looked like so many ants.

The camels halted. The camel drivers uttered commands, and the animals knelt, going down front legs first. Tom was prepared this time, and held on tight. Even so, he felt himself being slung forward as the camel descended.

They dismounted. The camels and their owners trotted away in search of customers for a return trip. Tom stared up at the pyramids.

He tried to imagine how it had been in the days of the three great pharaohs, Khufu, Khafre, and Menkure, who had built these pyramids as monuments to their own greatness. He saw armies of sweating workmen, baking under the merciless sun, hauling the huge blocks of stone across the desert. He heard the crack of the whips, the harsh snap of the overseers' voices, the groans of exhaustion.

Then he heard a thin voice whine, "You want souvenir photos? Color pictures, one hundred mills for whole booklet. I take U.S. money, too."

"No, we——" Tom began.

"You need a guide? I show you the Sphinx, I show you many interesting things. You are Americans? I help you see the ancient greatnesses. Here. Book about Egypt, tell you where you see good things. Only one pound, two hundred mills—yes?"

"Thanks, but we'll manage without all that," Dave said.

"You do better with me," the guide persisted. He was a short swarthy man with crooked teeth and a long mustache, and he seemed almost comically eager to do business with them. His eyes sparkled as he hunted for something these two Americans would be willing to buy. "Maybe you want to take home Egyptian antiquities?" he suggested. "Real good souvenir, you bet. Dug up in tombs at Thebes. I give you good price. You do no better anywhere. I——"

Dave cut him off with a short sentence in Arabic. The guide blinked in surprise and his lower jaw sagged. Then he smiled and touched his hand to his brow in a quick salute. "Thank you," he said nervously. "I not bother you. Thank you. You forget what I say, yes? Thank you. Thank you so very. Thank you. Thank you." He scuttled away. Tom laughed. "What did you say to him?" he asked Dave.

"I told him I had a friend who was an inspector with the

Department of Antiquities in Cairo. He knows he can get arrested for peddling black-market relics to tourists. It's been a thriving business in Egypt for centuries. Find a tomb, break into it, sell its contents to tourists. The Egyptian government keeps cracking down."

"Do you really know an inspector?"

"Of course not. But at least it'll save us from being pestered by the guides. Take a look."

Tom glanced around. He saw the man who had approached them nudging one of his fellow guides. He was passing the word—stay away from the two Americans over there! Tom grinned as he saw the whispering spread.

It worked wonderfully well. No one else came near them as they toured the pyramids.

Tom and Dave drew close to one of the structures and watched a boy scramble up the big blocks of stone, moving at an astonishing clip. When he came down, a little breathless, he collected small coins from applauding sight-seers. Dave pointed to an opening about forty feet above the ground from which another boy had just emerged. "That leads to the inner passageways," he said. "A maze of chambers and dead-end trails."

"Can we go in?"

"There's nothing to see," Dave said. "Just dark tunnels leading nowhere."

Tom nodded. He knew already that the pyramids, though they had been built as tombs for the pharaohs, had not served their purpose well. The kings had gone to rest in their vast stone burying places, accompanied by fabulous treasure— but, thousands of years ago, thieves had entered the pyramids, perhaps after bribing the guards, and had made their way down the twisting inner passageways to plunder the treasure of the pharaohs. After a while, the kings of Egypt had stopped building pyramids altogether. So that their bodies could rest in eternal peace, they had taken to hiding their tombs in remote places.

Even then, the tombs had been robbed. But the thieves had had a more difficult time getting at their loot. Only once had a pharaoh's tomb remained unmolested until modern times, Tom knew. That was the tomb of Tutankhamen, the boy-king who had ruled about 3300 years ago. For some reason, the thieves had overlooked Tutankhamen's tomb, and archaeologists discovered it with all of its wondrous treasure intact. Tom had read about that. The tomb had been opened in 1922. He had seen photographs of the miraculous works of art that had been found in the young pharaoh's tomb— the golden masks that showed the dead king's handsome face, the jars of alabaster, the chariots and statuettes, the massive coffins.

What if some other tomb still lay untouched somewhere in Egypt? Tom wondered. What if it were found this very summer? Suppose he and Dave were lucky enough to be right on the scene as some new find, more spectacular even than that of the tomb of Tutankhamen, was made?

Tom smiled. It was only a dream. The odds against anything like that happening in the next two months were astronomical. But there was no law against dreaming, was there?

Dave tapped his elbow. "You awake?"

"Just daydreaming, Dave."

"This is the place for daydreaming, isn't it?" Dave asked. "What were you dreaming about?"

"Nothing. Just a daydream, that's all. Nothing important. Let's go look at the Sphinx."

Tom and Dave got back to Cairo late that night. Tom felt thoroughly dried out from his long day in the bright sunlight, and he drank what seemed like gallons of water back at the hotel. Before bedtime, they packed their things. In the morning they would leave Cairo, and begin their venture in the land of the pharaohs.

Tom studied the map as he lay in bed. In the past few weeks, since the Egyptian trip had materialized so unexpectedly for him, he had peered at the map hundreds of times—until its lines were engraved on his brain. But now he looked again, mentally tracing the route he would be taking with his uncle.

They would travel south partly by train, partly by boat. The first section of the journey would be made fairly rapidly. They could not possibly take in everything Egypt had to offer, so they would pass speedily over the first three hundred miles of their trip, making their first important stop at Thebes.

Thebes had been the capital of Egypt during its greatest days. Some of Egypt's most important monuments were at Thebes and at nearby Luxor and Karnak. He and Dave would spend a few days there. Then they would go onward, always staying close to the Nile—for Egypt was actually only a narrow ribbon of a country, a few miles wide and hundreds of miles long. The valley of the Nile *was* Egypt. Away from the river, there was nothing but desert and rock.

Tom and Dave would travel to Aswan, where the immense new dam was getting its finishing touches. On, southward, to Abu Simbel with its colossal statues of Rameses II, then across the border from Egypt to Sudan, into the upper reaches of the Nile. They were going to spend most of the summer eight hundred miles south of Cairo, living with a team of archaeologists who were working against time to excavate ancient ruins before the waters of the new man-made lake covered them.

Nubia was their goal, though it was on few modern maps. Nubia was the name for an area taking in much of Upper Egypt and Lower Sudan—where the people spoke the Nubian language instead of Arabic. Long ago, Nubia had been an Egyptian possession, so it was studded with the remains of Egyptian settlements. In the furnacelike dry heat, nothing ever rotted or decayed. Archaeologists could unearth things three or four thousand years old and find them as fresh and unchanged as if they had been buried the day before yesterday. Teams of archaeologists were working frantically in Nubia now, with time running out for sites which were close to the river. The dam was nearly finished. The water was rising rapidly.

Tom folded the map, put it aside, and lay back.

"What time's our train?" he asked.

"Early," Dave said. "And we'd better not miss it. We've got a busy day ahead of us."

"I guess we'll get to Thebes by nightfall, won't we?"

"Thebes? We aren't going to Thebes tomorrow."

"Isn't that our first stop?"

"Not any more," Dave said. "I've added a stop in between. Tell el-Amarna."

Tom frowned. The name was unfamiliar. He had pored industriously over the guide books and history books before leaving the States, but his head was crammed with so many Egyptian names, dates, and places that he was unable to keep them all straight.

"Tell el-Amarna," he repeated slowly. "Tell el-Amarna." Reaching again for the map, he unfolded it and ran his eye down the snakelike path of the Nile, checking the names of the settlements between Cairo and Thebes. "I don't see it on the map," he said after a moment. "How important can it be, if it isn't even on the map?"

"It's near Mellawi," Dave said. "Is Mellawi on your map?"

"Hmm—yes, here it is. About halfway from Cairo to Thebes."

"Tell el-Amarna's just across the river. It's got some very important ruins. The city founded by Akhnaten is there. Ring any bells?"

Tom thought a moment, trying desperately to sort his way through three thousand years of Egyptian history. "Yes," he said. "Akhnaten—wasn't he the one who tried to overthrow the old Egyptian religion? The pharaoh who wanted Egypt to worship a single god?"

"He's the one. One of the most interesting men in Egyptian history," Dave said. "He left Thebes and built a new capital for himself, where he could worship his new god, Aten, in his own way. That's where we're going tomorrow. Akhnaten's city. I couldn't let us skip it. We'll stop by and pay our respects to him."

CHAPTER THREE

THE CITY OF AKHNATEN

The train rolled along at an unhurried pace. They were traveling up the western bank of the Nile. From his seat at a left-hand window, Tom watched the steady flow of the river, so muddy here that it looked yellowish-brown. It was late June, and the Nile flood was just beginning.

Tom knew about the annual flood and its importance to Egypt. Each spring the rains began in the hills of Ethiopia where the sources of the Nile form. Slowly the water gathered, until, at last, it came rushing downriver through Sudan; then, in the summer, poured into Egypt, carrying with it an immense load of silt, decaying leaves, and stripped-away topsoil.

As the Nile coursed toward the Mediterranean, it dropped its load of silt and mud—spreading a fertile layer of soil many feet thick over the land along its banks. By October, the flood waters were gone, and the Egyptians sowed their crops. Under the warm sun, the plants sprang up almost without tending, nurtured by the rich mud of the Nile. There were two, sometimes three, harvests before the fierce heat of April and May put an end to the growing season. Then, in June and July, the cycle began again with the annual

23

flood which brought with it new fertility for the fields. That is why an ancient geographer wrote: "Egypt is the gift of the Nile."

But the Nile was not always generous. In some years, the flood was scanty and the fields remained dry. During those years, famine stalked the land. Children died; men and women grew gaunt; the hollow-bellied cattle and goats gave little milk.

The Aswan High Dam would end the fear of drought. Egypt had started to build it in 1960, half Tom's lifetime ago. It had taken until spring, 1964, to build the bypass canal which diverted the flow of the river and allowed the engineers to throw a dam across the dry bed of the Nile. Then construction of the huge dam itself had begun. More years had gone by; the dam was complete now except for the finishing touches. It lay like a collar of concrete across the throat of the Nile. Water was backing up south of the dam, forming a lake that would eventually be hundreds of miles long.

The artificial lake would be Egypt's vital reservoir. In years when the spring rains were light and the summer flood feeble, the reservoir could be opened, releasing water to irrigate the Egyptian fields. The dam would make possible the cultivation of a million acres of land that had been barren desert. Electricity generated by the hydraulic power station of the dam would help make Egypt a modern industrial nation.

But there was a price for all this progress, Tom realized. South of the dam in Nubia, entire villages had already been covered by the rising water. Thousands of people had had to leave the land where their forefathers had dwelled for centuries. The Egyptian government had paid their expenses and moved them north to the settlement of Kom Ombo. Their old homes were lost forever. Lost, too, were any archaeological treasures that were hidden by the sands of Nubia. Each day, the water rose a little higher, devouring a few more feet of Nubian land. Already, the region just south of Aswan was flooded. Time had not yet run out for Sudanese Nubia, where Tom and Dave were going. But even there few seasons were left before the waters of the lake would rise for good.

Sometimes the train veered away from the river, following an inland route into the cotton fields of the Nile valley. Since the train was half empty, Tom and Dave moved across the aisle for a better view of the fields and the desert beyond.

"There's the dividing line," Dave said. "On this side, the soil is black and rich. On the other side, it's red desert sand. Life here, death there."

"I didn't think it would be such a sharp line," said Tom. "You could stand with one foot on either side!"

It was true. The fertile black soil of the river valley met the barren sand of the desert west of the train tracks. It was the most vivid possible demonstration of Egypt's problem: ninety-nine percent of the people lived on three percent of the land. Only the narrow strip along the Nile could support life. The rest of the land was arid desert, inhabited only by wandering Arab tribes.

Tom squinted toward the desert. Desert dust came rolling across the train as sudden breezes swept over the dunes. Parched hills rose in the distance. And the sun, almost straight overhead now, beat down wickedly. Shimmering heat waves danced in the air.

25

"Mellawi's the next stop," Dave announced. "Let's get our things together."

The train jolted to a halt, and porters sang out the name of the station. About a dozen passengers got off—all of them tourists, it seemed. Tom and Dave found themselves standing beside their luggage at the station, while taxi drivers wigwagged for their attention.

"We have to hire a cab to take us to the river," Dave explained. "It's about half a mile."

"Why don't we just walk it?"

Dave laughed and pointed to the suitcases. "In this heat? We'll keel over after five minutes. You're in Egypt now, Tom. And it's summertime. Don't look for trouble."

The cab they hired was a venerable old rattletrap that looked as though it had been doing service almost since the time of the pharaohs. They were soon on their way, joggling down a dusty dirt road. It was the longest half-mile trip in Tom's memory; it seemed to last for hours. But finally they pulled up at the Nile. The river looked peaceful, sleepy. Tom glanced across its broad yellow expanse and saw handsome palm trees lining the bank on the opposite shore. Behind the palms were small mud-brick houses, and, a few miles beyond them, rose a wall of brown cliffs.

Several boats were waiting. Dave chose a boatman and they got aboard his craft. A leisurely journey took them to the far side of the river. They stepped ashore at the unimposing village of Tell el-Amarna.

Dave raised his arm in a broad sweeping gesture. "Here we are," he said grandly. "The city Akhnaten built. He called it 'The City of the Horizon of the Sun.' "

26

"Where is it?" Tom said, puzzled. "It can't be this little mud village."

"No, it isn't."

"Then—where——?"

"There isn't much left of it now," Dave said. "Akhnaten's enemies did a good job of destroying it. But we'll see what's here today. I think we'd better get ourselves a guide this time. We'll probably need one."

It was fairly easy to arrange for a guide. There were some villagers lounging around, ready to pick up a few easy mills by showing the strangers the ruins, but the Egyptian government had also set up a guide service. Dave quickly found one of the official guides. He was a sleek, plump-faced young man with large round eyes and an agreeable smile.

"I am Mahmoud Hassan," he said. "You wish me to speak English, French, Arabic, Greek, Spanish, Italian, German——?"

"English will be fine," Dave said.

"Are there any languages you *don't* speak?" Tom asked.

Mahmoud Hassan laughed amiably. "In the winter, we had Turks here. My Turkish is not so good, but they also spoke Greek. Two summers ago, there came a family of Brazilians. I have little Portuguese, but we were able to speak in Spanish." He clucked his tongue. "And then there are the Chinese. We get many visitors from China now. I think they come to keep an eye on our Russian friends who help us build the dam. I am learning Chinese now, but it is hard, hard! One cannot tell the story of this great pharaoh in sign language, however."

As he spoke, Mahmoud Hassan led Tom and Dave toward three waiting donkeys. They mounted the animals.

The guide explained: "The ruins stretch for some six miles along the river. But we will not see everything unless you insist. I must admit that what remains of the city is not greatly exciting to the eye—unless you are archaeologists. Are you perhaps archaeologists?"

"No," Dave said. "I'm a writer. I'm on my way to Nubia to watch the excavations in the flood region. And Tom goes to school."

"To the university?" Mahmoud Hassan asked.

"Not yet," Tom said. "Not for three more years."

"I have been to university," said the guide. "I studied in Cairo. History, languages, literature. All the official guides must have an education. It is the rule." They were plodding north now, a few hundred yards inland, keeping parallel to the river. There was not much to see, Tom thought. He caught sight of the stumpy foundations of buildings, rising a few feet above the sand, but there was nothing else.

The guide said, "All that you see here was once the city of Akhnaten. At this place, there is a plain curving away from the river for several miles, reaching to those cliffs. It is like the shape of your letter *D*. Akhnaten built his city along the river, along the straight side of the *D*. And out there in the hills, on the curve of the *D*, are the royal tombs."

"Is Akhnaten buried there?" Tom asked.

Mahmoud Hassan smiled. "You will know all the story in good time, my friend."

Tom felt a little embarrassed at having jumped the gun. Obviously, Mahmoud Hassan had developed his own way of showing the city to tourists, and did not want them to anticipate any part of it.

The donkeys jogged along. The guide said, "Akhnaten was

28

Egypt's king about the year 1370 before Christ. He became pharaoh when Egypt had a great empire. Everything to the south of this area belonged to Egypt, down to the southern part of what is now the Sudan. And the whole region of the Levant was Egypt's—the countries that now are Syria and Lebanon and Israel and Jordan. Akhnaten belonged to the Eighteenth Dynasty of Egypt's pharaohs. That is fairly late in Egypt's history, you understand. The pyramids at Gizeh were built by the kings of the Fourth Dynasty and were about fifteen hundred years old when Akhnaten became king."

Tom's head swam as he tried to come to terms with the immense spans of Egypt's history. Yesterday, he had seen the pyramids; today he was at Akhnaten's city. As much time had gone by between the building of the pyramids and the birth of Akhnaten as between the fall of the Roman Empire and the twentieth century. Even so, Akhnaten was a figure out of the incredible past. He had lived before the Trojan War, had lived before the founding of Rome, had lived before——

Tom felt dizzy. How did you comprehend the history of a nation that had lasted so many thousands of years?

Mahmoud Hassan was saying: "Akhnaten had a different name when he came to the throne. He was pharaoh— Amenhotep IV. The first part of his name honored the god Amon, who was Egypt's chief god then. There were many other gods, too. There was Re, the god of the sun, and Isis and Horus and Osiris, and Ptah, and Thoth, and hundreds of others besides. Each city of Egypt worshipped its own gods. But Amon was the chief god. He was the lord of Thebes, which was the capital of Egypt. Thebes is about two hundred and fifty miles south of here."

"We're going there tomorrow," Dave said.

29

"It is still a wonderful sight," said the guide. "But Amenhotep IV disliked Thebes. And he disliked Amon. Amon was a greedy god, a god who demanded tribute, a god who had to be worshipped in dark temples which made a man fearful. The priests of Amon were fat and rich. They were almost as powerful as the pharaoh himself. Amenhotep IV rebelled against Amon and all the other gods of Egypt. He declared that they were false gods, and he proclaimed a new god. *One* god. He ordered that Egypt would have a single god, a god of love and kindness." Mahmoud Hassan pointed straight up. "There is his god."

"The sun," Tom said.

"Yes. The sun. But he did not worship the sun itself, as a *thing*. He worshipped the glowing face of the sun—its light and warmth and brightness. Do you see the difference? He called his god 'Aten,' which was the Egyptian word for the face of the sun. And he changed his own name to Akhnaten, which meant 'He Who Serves Aten.' Akhnaten left Thebes and built a new capital here, where no one had ever lived before. These bits of brick, these broken ruins, are all that remain."

As the donkeys picked their way down what had probably once been a grand processional avenue, Mahmoud Hassan sketched in the story of Akhnaten. He described the way the rebellious pharaoh had sent agents through Egypt to close the temples of the other gods and destroy statues of them. Any inscriptions that mentioned the name of Amon were hacked from the walls. Only Aten could be worshipped. Akhnaten was the first man in history to worship one god instead of many gods.

The guide told how Akhnaten had dwelled happily at his city for many years with his beautiful wife Nefertiti and his growing family of young daughters. The king was surrounded by followers who accepted the new religion of Aten. Together with his friends, Akhnaten went each day to the temple of Aten to sing praise to his god.

"The temple was there," Mahmoud Hassan said. "We have traced its foundations. These low brick walls here are the ruins of Akhnaten's palace. Behind us is the town itself. Ahead, to the north, lies a suburb of the town. And at the very end of the plain is another palace where Queen Nefertiti spent much of her time."

Mahmoud Hassan explained that beyond Akhnaten's own city the new religion attracted few followers. The peasants of Egypt knew little about Aten, and clung to the gods they had long loved—Isis and Osiris and Horus. In Thebes, the priests of Amon schemed and plotted to overthrow the pharaoh and restore their own power. But Akhnaten did not pay attention to the mutterings of his enemies.

"He was interested solely in serving his god," said Mahmoud Hassan. "Atenism was a wonderful religion, a religion of kindness and tenderness. Some of its hymns have survived, and they are beautiful and touching. But, though he invented a good religion, Akhnaten was a poor ruler. He did not spend much time dealing with the problems of government. There were rebellions in the north, in Syria, Lebanon, and Palestine. Akhnaten did not send soldiers to put the rebellions down. Law and order were overthrown. Many insignificant princes set up tiny kingdoms. The Egyptians were driven out. While Akhnaten dreamed and prayed, the Egyptian empire fell apart. Tribute from the foreign lands stopped coming in. The wealth of hundreds of years of conquest was lost in a few short years."

"Didn't he realize what was happening?" Tom asked.

"Perhaps he did not care," answered Mahmoud Hassan. "Perhaps he did not enjoy making war. Aten was not a god of war. In many ways, the Aten religion was like Christianity. Akhnaten believed in peace, in the harmony of all things."

"He must have seemed very strange to the people of his day," Tom said.

"He was strange. He even *looked* strange," the guide agreed. "He had a very long head, a heavy chin. His body was crippled in some way, too. His legs were crooked and his thighs were swollen so that he could not stand straight. We know all this because Akhnaten insisted that his artists paint him exactly as he looked. All the other pharaohs, before and after, were vain men who wanted to be made more handsome than they actually were. Not Akhnaten. His portraits show his deformed body. Perhaps he had tuberculosis or some other disease."

"Was he overthrown by a revolution?" Tom asked.

The guide smiled mysteriously. "No one knows how Akhnaten died. He had been king for seventeen years—then, suddenly, he was king no more. He and Nefertiti simply vanished from history. A boy was put on the throne."

"Tutankhamen," Tom said quickly.

"Yes. Tutankhamen. Some say he was the younger brother of Akhnaten; others think he was Akhnaten's son. He was less than ten years old when he became king. He was married to one of Akhnaten's daughters. She was only eleven. Naturally, the young king and queen did not rule Egypt themselves.

32

Strong men ruled behind the scenes. A priest named Ay and a general named Horemheb were the actual rulers."

Mahmoud Hassan described the way in which all Egypt turned against Akhnaten's memory, now that he was dead. The man who had tried to abolish the ancient gods of Egypt was denounced as a traitor. Pharaoh Tutankhamen and the royal court moved the capital back to Thebes. Wrecking crews came to Akhnaten's city and destroyed it almost completely. Just as Akhnaten had once closed the temples of Amon and cut Amon's name off the inscriptions, so, now, the new rulers blotted out Akhnaten's name. Wherever a statue or a portrait of the dead king was found, the name of Akhnaten was chipped away. No one spoke of him any more except as "that criminal" or "that traitor." The man who had tried to give Egypt a beautiful new religion was wiped from history.

"He was not even listed in the roll of pharaohs," said Mahmoud Hassan. "Akhnaten was wiped out completely, as though he had never existed."

When he was about eighteen, Tutankhamen died. He was buried near Thebes with the pomp and splendor a pharaoh deserved. Ay, the fat priest, proclaimed himself king, though he was not of royal blood. He ruled a few years and died. Then General Horemheb took the throne. He, too, was a commoner, but he was the most powerful man in Egypt.

"After Horemheb died," Mahmoud Hassan went on, "a new royal family came to rule in Egypt. Their rule was known as the Nineteenth Dynasty. The most famous king of this dynasty was Rameses II. It was during the Nineteenth Dynasty that Moses led the Hebrews out of Egypt, so it is thought."

The guide fell silent. The donkeys halted. Sweltering under

33

the blazing sun, Tom gazed in somber fascination at the ruins of Akhnaten's city. Here, some thirty-three hundred years ago, a strange, deformed king and his beautiful queen had sung the praises of a god of love. Here chariots had flashed by, and swirls of incense had risen to the heavens, and slaves had bowed down to the pharaoh.

"We have come to the Northern Palace," said Mahmoud Hassan. "Only the foundations are left. Come. We will walk through the palace."

Tom tried to imagine himself in the palace as it had been, with a roof overhead to shield him from the giant blazing eye in the heavens. Once there had been pillars and colonnades here. There had been cool halls through which Akhnaten and Nefertiti had strolled. According to the guide, there had also been a zoo here with birds and beasts from many lands. Tom could imagine gardens of exotic plants bordering the palace which were kept green by the waters of the nearby Nile. Mahmoud Hassan gestured, outlining the foundations of what had been bedrooms, throne rooms, pavilions.

Gone. All gone. Akhnaten's enemies had done their work well. His splendid city had lasted only about twenty years. Then it had been shattered by men who hated the dead king and the religion he had tried to establish.

Mahmoud Hassan pointed to the cliffs, a few miles to the east. "Shall we visit the tombs?" he asked. "Or have you had enough?"

Dave looked at Tom. The decision was his. Back to the station to wait for the midday train? Or a broiling donkey ride to the distant cliffs?

"The tombs," Tom said. "By all means, let's go to the tombs."

The guide seemed pleased. He tugged at the reins of his donkey, and they began to plod toward the cliffs. As they drew closer, Tom saw a break in the cliffs, about halfway down the curve of the D. It was, Mahmoud Hassan said, a *wadi*—a stream bed which was dry except in the rainy season. The tombs of Akhnaten's city were in two groups, one south of the wadi; the other, north. The riders were heading for the southern group of tombs.

"There are nineteen tombs here," Mahmoud Hassan said. "They belong to the chief officials of the city. We have the tombs of Mahu, the chief of police; Apiy, the royal steward; and May, the royal chancellor. There is Horemheb's tomb, and the tomb of Ay. But few of these tombs were ever used. They were prepared in advance, for the Egyptians began building their tombs while they were still alive. Most of Akhnaten's friends and officials deserted his religion after the king died. They left Tell el-Amarna and built new tombs for themselves in Thebes. But these tombs were left untouched when the rest of the city was destroyed. Let us see them closer."

They left the donkeys at the base of the cliff and clambered up a steep-angled slope to a hole in the rock. Mahmoud Hassan led them in. Stepping from the fierce heat of the desert into the cool silence of the tomb was like jumping into a cold lake on a hot day. The difference in temperature was so great that Tom began to shiver at first; then he grew accustomed to it.

His eyes, too, had to adjust to his new surroundings. The inky darkness of the first few moments soon gave way to dimness. The guide flashed a light to help them see.

"Each tomb has about the same pattern," Mahmoud

Hassan explained. "There is a forecourt, a hall supported by columns of rock, then an inner chamber, and small adjoining rooms which would have been used to store articles that the soul of the dead man might need in the afterlife. We are in the tomb of Tutu, who was Akhnaten's Foreign Minister. You would say, his 'Secretary of State.' Tutu was in charge of dealing with other countries. Since Akhnaten was not interested in such matters, he left Tutu to act as he wished. We have found ancient letters which indicate that Tutu was a treacherous man who aided Egypt's enemies. But Akhnaten was fooled by him and thought he was good and wise."

There was a mural on the plaster wall of the tomb. Tom saw lines of elegant hieroglyphic inscriptions which Mahmoud Hassan said were the words of a hymn to Aten. He translated a few lines:

I come with praise to Aten, the living, the only god, lord of radiance, who makes light when he rises in heaven.

The mural showed Akhnaten—his head strangely elongated, his thighs swollen. He was certainly badly deformed, Tom thought, yet there was something noble and majestic about him all the same. By his side was Nefertiti, lovely, slender, and graceful. She held two babies on her knees. Other figures surrounded the royal pair. Mahmoud Hassan said that they represented ambassadors from Syria, Nubia, and other lands, bringing tribute to Egypt. The scene had been painted early in Akhnaten's reign, before the overseas empire had crumbled. And there was Tutu himself, bowing to the king. Painted around him in panels were lines of hieroglyphics.

"Tutu is praising Akhnaten," Mahmoud Hassan said. "He is telling the king how great he is. Of course, Tutu designed the murals in his tomb himself. He told his artists to compose words of praise for the ruler. But they were lying words. He thought Akhnaten was a fool. He did much to harm him."

They moved on to other tombs, well spaced along the wall of rock. The tomb of Mahu, the chief of police, showed Akhnaten riding in his chariot, holding the reins himself. Nefertiti and one of their daughters rode with him. A plump man trotted alongside the chariot, apparently having a hard time keeping up with it. It was Mahu himself, said the guide. The chief of police was evidently trying to tell the king something important, but Akhnaten had not slowed the chariot during the conversation.

The murals were bright, sparkling, full of life and wit. They were so fresh they seemed brand new, except that there were areas of damage on them, the wounds of time. Mahmoud Hassan pointed to an empty place on the wall. "That scene was destroyed a few years ago," he commented. "One of the men from the village was discharged from his job as a guard here. For revenge he came back and damaged that painting. He injured all the world that way, not only the man who fired him. We try to keep such things from happening, but it is not always easy. The villagers do not understand how precious these things are."

Tom stared in dismay at the lost mural. He felt cheated; it was unfair that such wonders should survive for thousands of years, only to be destroyed by petty spite later.

The party left Mahu's tomb, continuing southward along the cliffs. Each tomb had its gay murals, its portraits of king and queen. One showed Akhnaten at a window in his palace, showering gifts on a loyal official. The king, seated on a pile of brightly colored cushions, leaned forward casually. Another portrait of the king showed him with his arm resting lightly around Nefertiti's waist; king and queen smiled at one another with obvious love, while their daughters twined around their legs. In another tomb, Tom saw Akhnaten on a balcony, throwing necklaces of gold down to a delighted man standing in a courtyard. The man being honored was Ay, who one day would become pharaoh himself. Ay's tomb was the grandest of all that they had seen.

At last they had finished exploring the tombs. Dazzling images crowded Tom's mind. But he had not forgotten one important question.

"Where is the tomb of Akhnaten himself?"

Mahmoud Hassan smiled his mysterious smile again. "Four miles out in the wadi," he said. "It is all alone, perhaps the loneliest place on earth. Few go there. The murals have been badly damaged."

"And the mummy of the pharaoh?" Tom wanted to know. "Is it there?"

"No. Akhnaten was not buried in his city."

"Where, then?"

"We do not know. Perhaps his enemies destroyed his body and his actual tomb when Egypt turned against him. That was the worst thing that could happen to an Egyptian—for if his body were destroyed, he could not have an afterlife. It may be that Akhnaten's foes hunted for his resting place and violated it, burning his body or hurling it into the Nile."

"What a terrible thing to do to such a great man!" Tom said.

"There is another possibility," said Mahmoud Hassan. "It

might have occurred that Akhnaten's friends smuggled his body out of the city when he died, knowing the harm that might befall it. Perhaps they carried him far away, and buried him in a secret place where no one could find and desecrate his tomb. We may never know."

"If there is such a tomb, is there any chance of finding it?" Tom asked.

"It is not many years since Tutankhamen's tomb was discovered. Where there is one tomb, there may be others. But I do not think Akhnaten's tomb, if there is one, will ever be found. He will sleep on forever, poor sad man." Mahmoud Hassan patted the neck of his donkey. "Come. Let us leave, now. You have seen the city."

CHAPTER FOUR

THE TEMPLES OF AMON

By nightfall, Tom and Dave were in Thebes. Actually, they were in Luxor, on the east bank of the Nile. Luxor, Karnak, and Qurna were the three modern towns which had sprung up where the old Egyptian capital had stood. Karnak was also on the east side of the river and Qurna was on the west. The temples of Thebes were at Luxor; the huge graveyard, the City of the Dead, was across the Nile.

Tom was in a subdued mood as they checked into their large, impressive hotel at Luxor. He had said little during the long train journey from Akhnaten's city to Thebes.

"Tired?" Dave asked. "You ought to be. We've been on the go all day. Sun and heat and dust—it's enough to knock anybody out."

"It isn't just the trip," Tom said quietly. "I've been thinking. About Akhnaten, about Nefertiti. About everything we saw today. You don't usually think of Egyptian kings and queens as *people*. They're like statues, really. But Akhnaten seems different. I almost feel as if I got to know him today."

"He's got a personality, yes. Just about the only pharaoh who had. That's why he's so interesting. He's the pharaoh who rebelled against age-old traditions."

"And failed."

"Did he?" Dave asked. "Sure, his religious ideas died with him and his name was blotted out by jealous men. But his ideas weren't forgotten. We know more about him than about any other pharaoh. He still interests us today. Akhnaten has lived on and all the other kings of Egypt have turned into figures of stone."

"Do you think there's any connection between Akhnaten and the modern religions?"

"Hard to say. There's thirteen hundred years between Akhnaten and Jesus. But the idea of one god—maybe that stayed alive after Akhnaten was forgotten. We can only guess. Maybe there was a secret underground which went on worshipping Aten. Somebody's suggested that, you know. Possibly Moses was originally a follower of Akhnaten's religion, and he handed some of Akhnaten's ideas down to the Jews. Who in turn passed the notion of one god along to the Christians and the Mohammedans. So maybe Akhnaten is behind all three of these present-day religions. But it's all guesswork, Tom. We'll never know."

Yes, Tom thought. Guesswork. At a distance of thirty-three centuries, who could know the truth? Who could tell fact from fantasy?

It was hard for him to shake off his moodiness as he got ready for bed. The eerie, brooding figure of Akhnaten seemed to haunt him.

But the rebel pharaoh did not invade Tom's dreams. He was so tired that he did not dream at all. It had been a long day's travel, with hours spent aboard trains and other hours passed wandering through the ruins of Akhnaten's lost city. He settled back against his pillow; the bed was comfortable, for this hotel at Luxor was every bit as modern and plush as the one at Cairo had been. He closed his eyes.

Dave said something. The words were blurred and vague. Tom started to ask, "What was that?" But he got halfway through the first word and it turned into a yawn. He said no more.

Eight hours of sleep and a hearty breakfast—and Tom was ready to start all over again.

"What's on the schedule for today?" he asked.

"Feel like seeing some temples?"

"Why not?"

"Off we go, then."

The biggest and grandest of the temples at Luxor was practically next door to the hotel. It had been built by Akhnaten's father, Amenhotep III, and honored Amon, the god whom Akhnaten had defied. As he entered the temple, Tom could see why Akhnaten, with his love of sunshine and simplicity, had turned away from Amon.

The temple was gigantic, ponderous, gloomy. Massive columns, many times the height of a man, formed a huge courtyard. Earthquake, fire, and siege had damaged the vast building, but enough of it remained to suggest its original appearance. Tom's flesh crawled. This was a temple that dwarfed men; it made them feel like insects. It was not hard to picture the grim faces of the priests of Amon as they performed mysterious rites while terrified worshippers crouched beneath the immense columns.

It was all so different from Akhnaten's religion, with its feeling for sunlight and warmth. On the train the night before, Tom had read the words of one of Akhnaten's hymns to his god, and he had been struck by the tenderness of the poem:

> The birds flutter in their marshes,
> Their wings uplifted in adoration to Thee.
> All the sheep dance upon their feet,
> All winged things fly,
> They live when Thou hast shone upon them.

After spending a short while amid the awesome magnificence of the Luxor temple, Tom said, "Let's go, all right?"

"What's the hurry?"

"I don't like this place. It gives me the creeps."

"It's marvelous, though," Dave said. "It's probably the finest temple of its time. Look at those pillars! Look at that——"

"Okay, it's impressive," Tom admitted. "But we've seen it, haven't we? There's something dark and cruel and ugly about this temple."

Dave frowned. Then he gave Tom an odd look and said, "I think I know what the trouble is, nephew mine."

"What?"

"Akhnaten's made a convert out of you. This is Amon's temple! And you prefer Aten. Isn't that it? You don't like it here because you think Amon's still skulking around the place."

Grinning sheepishly, Tom admitted, "Maybe you're right. Anyway, can we go?"

Dave took a last look around, and they left. Their next port of call was a little more than a mile away—Karnak. They passed down a broad street which, according to Tom's guide-book, had once been an avenue lined with sphinxes.

As they came into Karnak, Dave said, "Here's something I know you'll like, Tom. *Another* temple of Amon. And this one's even bigger than the last one."

Tom felt a tremor of awe. Amenhotep III's temple at Luxor seemed almost quaint next to this monstrous place. He managed to keep his emotions under control this time, how-ever. He forced himself to forget the lonely pharaoh and his doomed religion, and to accept the temple at Karnak as the wonder that it was.

They roamed through the temple, which covered many acres—a confused jumble of ruins.

"Many pharaohs built temples here," Dave said. "Or re-built old ones. At first, Amon was an unimportant local god, but, when the capital was moved to Thebes, Amon began to need new and bigger temples."

"The capital was in the north before, wasn't it? Up near the pyramids?"

"That's right. In Lower Egypt. But about 2100 B.C. a new dynasty took charge—the Eleventh—and made Thebes the capital. And for the next fifteen centuries practically every pharaoh built something in honor of Amon here at Karnak."

"Except Akhnaten," Tom said.

"He built a temple here too," Dave said. "Before he moved to his new city. But it was a temple for Aten. That must have shaken things up in Thebes."

The main building, Tom learned from his guidebook, had been built by Thothmes I, a pharaoh who ruled early in the Eighteenth Dynasty. Not much of that temple remained. A courtyard separated it from a huge column that had been erected by Amenhotep III. Nearby, a double row of even more gigantic columns called the "hypostyle hall" had been built by one of the many kings named Rameses. Tom could not repress shivers as he walked between the enormous pillars of stone.

Beyond them lay an obelisk, a tall stone spike nearly a hundred feet high, topped by a pyramid-shaped point. On its pink granite sides were carved large hieroglyphic inscriptions.

"This is the obelisk of Queen Hatshepsut," Tom said after looking at the picture in his guidebook and comparing it with the monument before him. "Let's see—she was before Akhnaten, wasn't she?"

"About a hundred years before," Dave said. "She's another Egyptian with a personality. Hatshepsut was the wife of Thothmes II. He was a weakling, though, and she was actually the one who gave the royal orders. When he died, she grabbed the throne and made herself king."

"*King?*"

"That's what I said. In Egypt, only a man could rule. But Hatshepsut wanted the throne herself, so she took the title, 'Pharaoh.' In statues of her, she's shown wearing a false beard. She was king of Egypt for more than twenty years. Meanwhile, the rightful heir to the throne was kept cooped up, a prisoner in the palace. He was her nephew, the son of Thothmes II."

"Wait a minute," Tom said in confusion. "She was Thothmes II's *wife*. How could his son be her nephew?"

"She was also his sister," Dave said. "Egyptian kings usually married their own sisters. The king had to marry someone of

45

divine blood, and his sister was the closest available relative. Thothmes II had several wives, and the heir to the throne was born to somebody other than Hatshepsut. So she was the boy's aunt, and maybe also his stepmother—but not his mother. Follow?"

"I think so," Tom said. "What happened to him?"

"He outlasted Hatshepsut. When she died, he came out of his palace and made himself king at last, as Thothmes III. He turned out to be one of Egypt's greatest pharaohs. He built the empire that Akhnaten later fizzled away."

Dave pointed to the inscription on the side of the obelisk. "Hatshepsut told her story on this obelisk. When her nephew became pharaoh he went around chopping her inscriptions up, but the priests wouldn't let him deface anything here in the temple. So he built a wall around the obelisk to hide Hatshepsut's story. The wall eventually crumbled, though. See that section there? Where three or four hieroglyphics are enclosed in an oval? That's the royal name. It's called a *cartouche*. Royal names were always written in cartouches, to show their importance. Whenever you see an oval like that, you know it contains some big shot's name."

"How do you keep all these royal families straight?" Tom asked, perplexed.

Dave winked. "I've been doing my homework, that's how."

They peered at Queen Hatshepsut's obelisk a few minutes longer. It was just a slab of stone, Tom thought. Yet it told a story of family feuds, of rival monarchs, of a queen who became a king and made Egypt accept her rule for twenty years. They were dead and gone, all of them, turned to dust centuries ago unless their mummies had survived. Yet here in the timeless land of Egypt it was almost as if their struggles had taken place the previous day.

Luxor and Karnak kept them busy all day. Tom's distaste for the ponderous temples of Amon vanished, and he roamed the mighty avenues with eager curiosity. He and Dave were far from alone. Tourists by the hundreds picked their way through the awe-inspiring ruins. Many of them, like Tom and Dave, traveled independently, using pocket guidebooks to give them information about what they were seeing. Others had hired local guides, as Tom and his uncle had done at Tell el-Amarna. Still others, in groups of fifteen or twenty, were shepherded along by tour leaders who rattled off brisk descriptions in German, or French, or English—depending on the nationality of the group. Tom half expected to see the sinister-looking Paul Kurtz appear, leading his camera-toting flock, but there was no sign of him.

The next day, Tom and Dave crossed the Nile to view the City of the Dead.

They made the same westward journey that mourning Thebans had taken in long-ago funeral processions. Up they went, into the bleak, wind-swept hills where many of the great people of Egypt had been laid to rest. They entered the Valley of the Tombs of the Kings, where, a thousand years after the time of the pyramid builders, the pharaohs had hidden their burial places.

Tom and Dave entered the tomb of Rameses VI. An inclined passageway led downward into chambers cut from stone. As at Akhnaten's city, the tomb walls were bright with murals—but the artistic style here was stiff and formal. There was none of the keen delight in humor and realism that the artists of Akhnaten had shown.

Nothing remained in the tomb but the paintings and carvings. Thieves had cleaned out the treasures of the dead centuries ago. Tomb after tomb in the valley revealed the same story of robbery and plunder. The gold of the pharaohs had proven so strong a temptation that not even the tomb guards had been able to resist it.

"Here's the only tomb that came down to us with its treasure intact," Dave said. "The tomb of Tutankhamen. Though even his tomb wasn't entirely untouched. It was broken into right after the king's funeral, but the thieves were caught and the tomb sealed up. No one entered it again until 1922."

"Why did his tomb escape?"

"Because Tutankhamen was such an unimportant king. He died young. People forgot about him. Since he was a relative of Akhnaten's, no one spoke of him. Thieves didn't know the tomb was there to be looted. Even the archaeologists who found it weren't sure there was such a tomb at all—until they stumbled upon it."

It was a small tomb, very deep in the ground. The passageway that led to it ran right underneath the tomb of Rameses VI. Tom was disappointed. There was nothing but a few small, empty rooms. He knew that the fabulous treasures of Tutankhamen were at Cairo, in the museum. Even so, he had thought that some sort of romantic excitement would still pervade Tutankhamen's tomb. He had been wrong.

On their way back from the Valley of the Tombs of the Kings, Tom and Dave visited the imposing temple of Queen Hatshepsut, which was built against a cliff that faced Karnak across the river. It was a handsome building indeed, with its long row of pillars running along the face of the cliff. Once again, Tom thought of the defiant queen who had donned a false beard to rule as king.

Then it was time to leave Thebes. They had not really dug deeply into the sprawl of temples and monuments there, but Nubia was calling. Tom was not sorry to go. The pillars and obelisks of Thebes were magnificent and striking, but they had the chill of death about them. A few temples, a few tombs, and he was ready to move along. Far to the south, he knew, they would be living in a small Nubian village, watching archaeologists at work making new discoveries. That was more attractive to him than staring at these eye-numbing piles of stone.

They boarded a Nile steamer at Luxor and moved at a dignified pace upstream. The river was incredibly broad beyond Thebes, sometimes as wide as two miles across. Its banks were lined with villages and farms, set well back from the edge of the river. Already, the first waters of the annual flood were beginning to lap at the farm fields. Rich silt would soon be deposited, making the fields fertile for the long season of growth. On both sides, beyond the inhabited zone, lay deserts and mountains.

Tom sat on the deck of the steamer, thumbing through his guidebooks and his Egyptian history book. Egypt was becoming so much clearer to him now than it had been back home when he first looked at them. Then, strange names like "Amenhotep" and "Hatshepsut" and "Horemheb" had been only a jumble of sound to him. Now he could match names and events—even faces. He could picture Horemheb, the tough general, supervising the destruction of Akhnaten's city.

He could see Akhnaten himself, sad-eyed and long-jawed; and lovely Nefertiti with her neck like a swan's; and handsome, tragic young Tutankhamen; and defiant Queen Hatshepsut wearing her false beard of monarchy.

They were approaching the southern border of ancient Egypt. Aswan marked the place where Egypt had ended and Nubia began. The river narrowed. Towering hills of granite loomed in the desert.

"There's the Aswan Dam," Dave said. "The old Aswan Dam, the one that's out of date now."

"It looks plenty big to me."

"Not big enough for Egypt's needs, though."

They toured the old dam which had been erected at the beginning of the twentieth century. A guide rattled off the statistics: completed in 1902, twice enlarged since, 176½ feet high, a mile and a quarter long, built of the same granite as the famous obelisks. But not even the guide could seem enthusiastic. "Have you seen the new dam yet?" he asked. "This is nothing. Nothing!"

Tom had to agree when he came to the Aswan High Dam, four miles to the south. There it was—El Sadd-el-Aali as the Egyptians called it—spanning the Nile from shore to shore. They looked down on it from a cliff, watching workmen toiling far below. The body of the dam itself was finished. The hydroelectric generators were now being installed and the inner mechanical parts of the dam were approaching completion. More than half a mile long at the crest, more than twice as high as the old dam, it was the most awesome of all the man-made works Tom had seen so far in Egypt.

An Egyptian in Western business clothes who stood near them on the observation platform seemed to think so too.

Pointing at El Sadd-el-Aali, he said quietly, "It is seventeen times as massive as the Great Pyramid. Imagine! Seventeen times as massive!"

Because it was the beginning of the flood season, the water level in the reservoir was low. But the lake that spread out south of the dam was huge nevertheless, and it was possible to see the mark on the cliffs where the water had reached during the high water of the previous year. This year the level would probably be even higher, for the rains had been heavy in Ethiopia, and the summer flood was off to an early start.

Tom and Dave did not linger long in Aswan. Soon they were aboard a new steamer, bound for the south. For the first part of the voyage, they traveled on the new reservoir. It did not seem as though they were on a river. The shores were distant, the water lapped at the cliffs. Then the lake narrowed to the shape of a river.

"We're passing over dozens of villages," Dave said. "Some that were drowned by the old dam, many more drowned by the new one."

"It must be hard on the people," Tom said. "Every few generations they have to scramble out of the way of a new lake that floods their land."

"There are always hard choices to make. Egypt needs these dams. But someone has to suffer so that the whole nation can go forward."

Tom nodded and walked to the deck rail. He peered down, into the brown, muddy depths of the Nile. He imagined that he could see waterlogged palm trees and swamped villages down there. What would the pharaohs, those mighty builders, have thought of El Sadd-el-Aali? Tom wondered. Seventeen Great Pyramids rolled into one! They would have laughed and refused to believe such things were possible.

There were monuments down there too, temples and tombs. Drowned, all drowned. And others yet to go under, Tom thought, as the steamer forged ahead, carrying him deeper and deeper into Nubia.

CHAPTER FIVE

WELCOME TO NUBIA!

They called the steamer an express! Tom wondered what the local could be like, since the big boat crawled along at such a torturously slow pace.

"Why didn't we take the railroad for this stretch?" Tom asked.

"Because there isn't any," Dave said. "Good enough reason?"

"About the best, I guess."

"Relax. Read. Sunbathe. Things are not hurried in Egypt. The country's been here for thousands of years, and no one's in a rush."

Tom settled back restlessly in a deck chair. The river was changing here, he saw. The eastern bank was rimmed with mountains that came down to the edge of the water, leaving little room for cultivation. On the western side, the hills were lower and further back, but the desert nearly touched the shore. Most of the settlements were on the mountainous eastern bank. Where the cliffs yielded to create a little pocket of fertile land, a village had sprung up. The western side, with its shifting desert sand, was evidently too tough a proposition

53

for cultivation. But the rising waters of the new lake would change all that, Tom knew.

It seemed as though weeks were going by on board the steamer. But they were really only a couple of days out of Aswan when they came to Abu Simbel, over a hundred and seventy miles up the river. One of Egypt's most famous monuments was there: the mammoth shrine built in his own honor by Rameses II, thirty-two hundred years before. Four great seated figures, two of them shattered and two intact, had originally been carved at the base of a cliff close to the edge of the Nile. The artificial lake soon would rise more than a hundred feet above the place where the six-story-high statues of Abu Simbel had been. But the skill of engineers had rescued the monument. Cut free from its backdrop of rock and raised to higher ground, it looked down now on the waters lapping at its base.

An afternoon at Abu Simbel—and then onward, southward.

"Say goodbye to Egypt," Dave remarked. "We're about to enter Sudan."

Nothing had changed but the name of the country. The steamer glided placidly along the river. They stopped at Wadi Halfa, just inside the Sudanese border, for a check of traveling papers. Tom examined his map.

"We're coming to the Second Cataract," he said.

"I doubt that we'll see it. It's another victim of the dam," said Dave.

Tom had learned that the course of the Nile went through a valley bordered by soft sandstone cliffs. However, at certain places along its route, the river had cut down into the hard granite deep below its bed. These upthrusting fangs of granite created dangerous rapids, the Nile cataracts, which once had been grim barriers to navigation.

The First Cataract was just above the first, or old, Aswan Dam. The Second Cataract was a few miles south of Wadi Halfa. Beyond lay the Third, the Fourth, the Fifth, and the Sixth Cataracts. Nubia was considered to be the area from the First Cataract south to a point midway between the Third and Fourth. Tom and Dave were bound for a town just above the Third Cataract.

"Listen to this," Tom said. He consulted his guidebook. "The Egyptians built a canal through the First Cataract about 2000 B.C. But it was five hundred years more before they could get their shipping through the Second Cataract. Once they did, they conquered southern Nubia. The Second Cataract stretches for about one hundred and thirty-five miles, and a hundred miles of it has so many rock outcrops and little islands that it's known as the Batn-el-Hagar, which means Belly of Stones."

Dave smiled. "But it isn't there any more."

It wasn't. The reservoir of the new dam had drowned the Second Cataract, had swallowed the Belly of Stones. The guidebook told of stony outcroppings in the river, an awful desolation of tumbled rocks. Yet the steamer went serenely on, heedless of the once deadly barriers now far below the surface of the river.

The lower slopes of the western cliffs were cloaked by drifts of bright yellow sand. On the east rose naked black rocks, and villages were occasionally scattered among them. In some places, the rock walls towered high above the river. They came to Semna, where two big granite forts still loomed above

55

the water, one on the east, and one on the west side. In the days of the Twelfth Dynasty, when the river had been only a hundred feet wide at this point, these two forts had completely commanded the area. No boat could pass without official permission. Thus had the pharaohs guarded their frontier.

Onward. Onward into Nubia.

Soldiers of the pharaohs had marched through this valley. Nubia was a gateway land, lying between North Africa and the darker, hotter lands south of the Sahara. Wars had been waged here. Tom read a 4,600-year-old battle report of Pharaoh Snefru: "The land of Nubia hacked to pieces; 7,000 men and women and 200,000 cattle and sheep led away."

Nubia's villages had yielded a harvest of slaves for Egypt. Nubia's quarries and mines had given up gold and precious stones. Traders had come south with wheat, honey, and textiles, and had gone north again bearing jungle goods: ivory, panther skins, ebony.

There was history here. It was not the overwhelming history of Thebes, with its ponderous monuments and towering temples. It was less visible. One had to dig deep to find it. It was the five-thousand-year record of man's struggles and accomplishments in Nubia, the comings and goings of warriors and merchants, the day-by-day toil of the villagers.

The Nile was cutting south and west through the Sudanese desert. Sandstone cliffs and tawny sand drifts still squeezed the river on both sides. Here, the effects of the new dam were yet to be felt. When it was full, the reservoir would be approximately 350 miles long and, in places, 16 miles wide. Here, though, more than 250 miles south of Aswan, it would be several more years before the water penned up behind the dam succeeded in flooding the ancient shores.

The long journey was almost over now. Tom watched village after village go by—Aksha, Kosha, then Abri—and wondered when they would come to their goal. The tiny villages, fringed by overhanging palms, huddled together, tucked away at the foot of the cliffs. Their little crescent beaches were green with low shrubbery that had a spiky, thorny look.

Ignoring the ferocious heat, Tom prowled the steamer's deck even through midday, roaming back and forth like a trapped panther. His uncle watched him with some amusement. Dave spent most of his time out of the sun, tapping away at his portable typewriter, starting the articles he had to write.

"Take it easy," he said. "We'll get there!"

"When?" Tom demanded.

"Oh, any year now. Sit down and read a good book. Study Nubian history."

"No, thanks. I've got the fidgets. I half feel like jumping overboard and taking a swim. This steamer is so slow I could probably keep up with it without even getting winded."

Somehow Tom controlled his impatience. If there had been someone besides Dave for him to talk to aboard the steamer, it might have helped. But the vessel had let practically all its passengers off at Abu Simbel or Wadi Halfa. The only travelers were some Sudanese businessmen who spent all their time talking business, loudly and rapidly, in a mixture of Arabic, French, and several other languages which Tom could not even begin to identify. They were probably headed for Dongola, an important town south of the Third Cataract.

Tom did not feel much like swimming, despite his words.

Crocodiles and large lizards lay sunning themselves on the shoals and sandspits near shore. That did not discourage the Nubians, for again and again Tom saw laughing brown-skinned children run down to the shore, free themselves of their single cotton garments, and leap gaily into the water. But he did not care to tempt the crocodiles, no matter how sleepy they looked.

There were birds everywhere, too, wheeling and shrieking, doubling back and forth across the river. Wild ducks and geese swooped low over the steamer, their wings brilliant hues of blue and green. High in the cloudless sky, larger birds went by in flocks, storks and cranes bound for lusher lands.

Finally, the steamer pulled toward shore.

"Delgo," Dave said. "We're here. Or almost here. We'll have to ride a few miles to the actual site."

"Do they know we're coming?"

"I wired ahead from Wadi Halfa. They'll probably meet us at the pier."

Tom and Dave were the only passengers who went ashore. It was early afternoon and the sun seemed to take up half the sky. Tom didn't even want to guess at the temperature; it was well over 100°, he was sure of that. But a wind out of the north moved the air around, making the heat a bit more tolerable.

Here, beyond the usual tourist haunts, no army of eager native guides came forward as the two Americans appeared. A few villagers peered shyly at them, but no one advanced. The pier was deserted. Thebes, with its bustle of tourists, its vast monuments, its luxurious hotels, seemed millions of miles away, not merely five hundred.

Then, a weather-beaten jeep pulled up on the shore and a

man jumped out. He was long and lean, well over six feet tall, with arms and legs so spindly that he looked more like a spider than a man. He wore khaki shorts and a white blouse open at the throat; wherever his skin was exposed, it was deeply tanned to a fine mahogany. A pith helmet crowned his head. When he took it off for a moment to fan himself, he revealed his thick, tangled reddish hair.

"Hello!" he called. "Are you the Lloyds?"

"You guessed it," Dave said.

The man came toward them. He walked in such a shambling, loose-jointed way that Tom corrected his earlier impression: he was less like a spider than a camel. His face was ugly in a good-natured way, with a big beak of a nose and a chin that tended to vanish below his mouth. A light dusting of freckles covered his skin. He was smiling broadly, and when he reached Tom and Dave he held out both hands at once, one for each of them.

"Did you have a good trip?" he asked.

"Peaceful," Dave said. "I'm David Lloyd, and this is my nephew Tom."

"A pleasure to meet you both." He spoke English in a curious way, not so much with an accent as without one, shaping each word neatly and cleanly. "I'm Kees van Vlaardingen. If you'll hop in, I'll take you out to the digs. And welcome to Nubia, both of you. Welcome to Nubia!"

It was a hot bumpy ride—but hot bumpy rides were getting to be familiar. Kees van Vlaardingen had tossed their luggage into the back seat of the aging jeep, and the three of them crowded into the front. When he put the jeep into gear, the shift creaked as though in protest.

59

"Our site is a few miles down the river," Kees said. "In the suburbs of Delgo, one might say."

"Have we missed much?" Dave asked.

"Oh, you've missed a lot of dull work. Gathering bits of pottery, that sort of thing. But there was a little excitement last week. It might lead to something, and, then again, it might not."

Tom felt sudden tension. "Something big? Something really important?"

"We cannot know that yet," Kees said. "What we have found is the entrance to an underground passageway. We struck it by accident the other Tuesday. It could be anything, you understand. Perhaps an ancient storeroom, perhaps somebody's wine cellar—or even a tomb."

"Are you going to explore it?" Tom asked eagerly.

"We hope to," Kees said. "But we are rather at a standstill now. We are simply looking longingly at our entrance, but we cannot do a thing. You see, the passageway runs right under the heart of the village. The villagers do not like us tunneling under their homes."

"Can't they be persuaded to let you work?" Dave wanted to know. "If you show them that there isn't any danger——"

"It is not so easy. They are a worried people. Already they know that many other villages down the river have had to be evacuated because of the dam. They do not fully trust us, and I think some of them believe we are engineers surveying for a new dam to cross the Nile at Delgo. So we are—how shall I say?—stymied. They watch the entrance to the passageway and forbid us to enter."

"But you're archaeologists," said Tom. "You aren't building any dams!"

"Of course, but how can we convince them?" Kees asked. "We can simply wait, that is all. Sheikh Ibrahim will be returning soon. He is the headman of the village, and he understands the purpose of our work. He is very intelligent. But he is in Cairo, and he will not return for several days. When he comes, we hope he will speak to his people and get permission for us to work. Without his help, we are blocked. The one thing we must not do is dig where the villagers do not want us to dig."

Very diplomatic, Tom thought. The archaeologists were here as guests of the village; they couldn't very well disturb the town against the will of its inhabitants. But what if Sheikh Ibrahim said *no*? Would they have to leave the mysterious, tantalizing passageway unexplored?

What if it contained something of spectacular importance? Tom wondered. If the villagers stood in the way, blocking the archaeologists, while time ran out and the waters rose, some priceless discovery might be lost for all time.

But Kees did not seem particularly troubled. Evidently, he had faith in Sheikh Ibrahim. Tom settled back, telling himself that he had to learn to keep his imagination under control. Quite likely the passageway was nothing more than an ancient sewer, or, as Kees had suggested, it led to a storeroom.

The jeep bumped along. Harsh winds scooped up hot sand and flung it against the windshield. Tom squinted to protect his eyes. There was no road, just a sort of camel track parallel to the Nile. There had been no houses for more than a mile, but, as they continued, the track veered closer to the river and patches of cultivated land appeared. Soon they were drawing into another village.

The houses were of mud brick, like the adobe buildings of

the American Southwest. The house walls were brown and lumpy, and it seemed to Tom as though one good downpour would melt the whole village away. But, of course, it almost never rained in Nubia, so the houses were safe. Their roofs were of thatched straw. The walls were freely decorated with ornaments painted in white plaster on the brown mud. In his first glimpse, Tom saw paintings of ships and fish, of birds and camels, palm trees, suns, moons, stars, flowers. There were crisscrossing geometrical patterns, complicated traceries of white.

"Our headquarters are at the north end of the village," Kees explained. "On the desert side. That is where we have done most of our work."

They rumbled through the center of the village. Curious Nubian children toddled out to look at the newcomers, but women and older girls hurried into the buildings.

"They are shy, afraid of strangers," Kees said. "They fear you will try to take their photographs. That is against the custom here."

"Where are the men?" Tom asked Kees. "Working in the fields?"

"No. At this time of the year, there is nothing to do in the fields. The growing season is over, and it will not be time to plant the new crops until after the summer. Most of the men have gone away to work in big cities. Some go north to Cairo; others, south to Khartoum. They come back when it is planting time."

He waved toward the houses. The squat mud buildings did not seem to have any windows except for tiny slits near the roofs, but Tom caught sight of the women and girls peering

62

cautiously from the doorways. He smiled at a girl; instantly, her head popped out of sight.

The people in Nubia were different from the Egyptians in appearance, Tom noticed. Most of the Egyptians had Arab blood, so usually they had sharp noses, thin lips, and swarthy but light skin. The Nubians were much darker, some of them so black they looked almost purple. Yet they did not have the blunt noses and full lips and woolly hair of Negroes. They were a mixed race, it appeared, bearing traces of invasion from both north and south. Arab features and Negro coloring combined to make the Nubians look unusual.

The jeep did not come to a halt until it had passed almost through the village. Kees braked sharply and the wheels kicked up clouds of sand. "There are five or six empty houses at the north end of town," he said. "We have rented them for the summer. Come and meet everyone."

He honked the horn loudly three times. Then they got out of the jeep.

The other members of the archaeological expedition began to appear. It was an international expedition, Tom knew. Right now there were dozens of archaeological groups working in Egypt and Nubia which had been sent from universities all over the world to carry out last-minute explorations before the dam waters flooded the area. This expedition had been sponsored jointly by an American and a German school. The archaeologists themselves came from many countries. On the ride from Delgo, Kees had revealed that he was from the Netherlands. He had been born in Amsterdam.

"Kees is only a nickname," he had explained. "It is short for Cornelius, but don't ever call me that, please!"

63

Six people had emerged from the mud huts at the sound of the horn. There were four men and two girls. They all looked fairly young and were smiling warmly. All were dressed in shorts, shirts, and pith helmets.

Kees said, "This is Dave and Tom Lloyd who will be staying with us for a while, as I think you know." Quickly, he made the introductions. The short blond man with the pale blue eyes was Helmut Blum, from West Germany, a photographer. Next to him was a long-legged girl, also fair-haired, from Sweden: Ursula Anderson. Kees said that she was an expert on Nubian pottery. Standing very close to Ursula was a big raw-boned man, Holger Carlson, from Denmark, who was introduced as an architect. The other three were American graduate students in archaeology: Janet Barker and Roy Fulton from Philadelphia, and Ted Clay from Salt Lake City. Janet was slender and appeared fragile; Roy, plump and perspiring; Ted, slim and muscular.

Holger Carlson asked, "You didn't see Sheikh Ibrahim get off the boat with them, did you?"

"No such luck," Kees said. "He won't be back ahead of schedule."

"It's hard to be patient," said Janet. "Have you told them about the trouble, Kees?"

"Yes. They know all about it. Where's Dr. Falke? He'll want to meet our new friends."

"In the administration hut," said Helmut Blum. "He's going over the aerial photos."

Kees beckoned to Tom and Dave, who followed him around one of the mud huts and through a doorway. They passed behind a high wall, and Tom saw why the Nubian houses did not bother with windows. The rooms were arranged around

64

an inner courtyard. A Nubian looked inward to his courtyard, not outward to the street. The squarish one-story rooms branched off from the courtyard. Kees strode into one of the rooms from which voices could be heard.

Three men sat around a table examining a thick sheaf of glossy photographs. They seemed to be older than the six archaeologists who had come out to meet Tom and Dave by the jeep. It was not hard for Tom to guess who the person in charge was. A dark-haired, powerful man sat facing the door. He had the widest shoulders and the deepest chest Tom had ever seen; he looked more like a weight-lifter than an archaeologist. He seemed gigantic, and the impression of great size was heightened by the bushy black beard which covered most of his face.

"Dr. Falke——" Kees said.

The men at the table looked up. A smile appeared on the face of the bearded man, two rows of bright white teeth emerging suddenly from the lush foliage of the beard.

"Ah! David!" he said, his voice booming basso profundo. "At last you are here!"

Dave stepped forward. Tom, a little overwhelmed by the physical presence of the expedition leader, hung back a pace or two.

Dr. Ludwig Falke got to his feet, and produced a new surprise as he did so.

He was short. Sitting down, Dr. Falke had seemed to be at least six feet four. But his brawny shoulders and great barrel of a chest had been joined, through some prank of nature, to short stubby legs. He was a fairly big man even so, but he stood no more than five feet ten, Tom's own height. Tom had expected to have to look up at him.

65

Dr. Falke stepped out from behind the table and reached for Dave's hand. "So good to see you again, David. So very good! And you are Thomas?" he rumbled.

Tom managed to conquer his sudden and unexpected shyness. "That's right, Dr. Falke." He put his hand forward and it was swallowed up by the archaeologist's massive paw. The handshake was bone-mangling. Tom tried not to wince.

Two years before, Dave Lloyd had met Dr. Falke at an archaeological expedition in Lower Egypt near the ancient city of Memphis. Dave had been sent to Egypt by a magazine to do a short piece on the diggings there, and at first Dr. Falke had not been at all happy to have an American journalist tagging around his site. But Dave had impressed the German archaeologist with his knowledge of Egyptology and his familiarity with Egyptian history. By the end of Dave's three-week stay, he had been accepted as almost a member of the expedition. So, when Dave had received his current assignment to write about the archaeological work in Nubia, it had not been hard for him to get Dr. Falke's permission to join his group—and even to bring his young nephew along.

"My colleagues," Dr. Falke said, talking so loud it seemed that the vibrations of his voice would knock the mud walls down. "To my left, Dr. Richard Marshall of Chicago. To my right, Dr. Heinrich Decker of Heidelberg. At the moment, you find us looking at bird's-eye-view photos taken from a helicopter late last month. Perhaps you know that buried archaeological sites are sometimes easy to see from the air—although invisible from the ground level. The earth is disturbed, and this disturbance is sometimes evident in a photograph taken from above. We are searching for new sites, since, as you may have heard, we are at the moment stopped here in the village. Kees, has there been further word about Sheikh Ibrahim?"

The lanky Hollander shook his head negatively. "He's expected next week, that's all."

Dr. Falke scowled. "We are all trying to be very patient, David. Here we sit with something perhaps quite important to investigate—and our hands are tied. We can do nothing until the Sheikh returns." His heavy brows knitted tensely. Then his face cleared. "But you two must be tired after your long trip. Kees, will you show them to their quarters? You can refresh yourselves. Tomorrow we will show you our work."

CHAPTER SIX

RUINS AND RIDDLES

The room which would be their home for the weeks to come was a good deal less than palatial, Tom thought. Still, he had been disappointed to find the hotels at Cairo and Luxor so American. Now he had a chance to live as the natives did—in a single mud-walled room.

It seemed like fun. The room was cool, at least by comparison with the outdoor temperature. Kees had said that the thermometer had hit 118° in the shade at noon that day, and Tom wasn't at all surprised. Instead of the straw mattresses the Nubians used, Tom and Dave had been given two folding cots as beds. A basin of water for washing and a pitcher of water for drinking stood near the wall. For bathing, Kees said, there was the Nile—but he recommended it only in the early morning and late afternoon, when the sun was less likely to roast their tender skins.

"No matter how tanned you get," he warned them, "you never get tanned enough. You must keep yourself covered in the middle of the day. A hat, always."

Since there was little furniture in the room besides the cots and a single table, they did not unpack their suitcases, but

68

simply took fresh clothes out and changed. The laundry, Kees told them before he left, was done in the village. As for cooking, members of the expedition took turns at that.

"We are not proud of our cooking," Kees said, "but no one has starved to death among us yet. Perhaps you will lend us your skills, if you have cooking abilities."

"Do Ursula and Janet do most of the cooking?" Tom asked.

Kees guffawed, clutching his lean belly and nearly doubling up. He recovered after a moment and said solemnly, "They are the only members of the expedition who are never allowed to serve as cooks."

"I thought all girls were good cooks," Tom said.

Kees still looked amused. "These two are archaeologists first and girls second. I suppose they will get married some day. Their husbands had better have stomachs of iron—or else enough money to hire a chef."

Tom felt excitement stirring in him as he rinsed away the dust of the journey. At last, they were with the expedition, no longer wandering around like wide-eyed tourists. He had liked the ten archaeologists immediately. Dr. Falke seemed a bit forbidding at first, but he was really not too terrifying. The others were relaxed and friendly. He couldn't wait to see them at work. And he could tell, from the way they kept bringing up the subject of Sheikh Ibrahim and his eagerly awaited return, that they were all eager to find out what might be hidden in the passageway beneath the town.

Tom poured himself a drink of water. Dave said, "Make mine water too."

"Coming right up, sir."

"Thanks." Dave gulped the water. "Well? Glad you didn't feed yourself to the crocodiles now? It was worth waiting for, wasn't it?"

"You bet it was. Dave, what'll happen if Sheikh Ibrahim doesn't let them go into the passageway?"

"They won't go, that's all," Dave said simply.

"Can't they order the natives to stand back? I mean, it's an emergency, with the water rising all the time——"

"This is their town," Dave said. "At least until the dam drives them out. Dr. Falke and his people are guests here. How would you like it if a bunch of Nubian archaeologists came to the United States and began ripping up your front yard? Dr. Falke has to go very gently here. The government gave him permission to dig, but only where he can get the cooperation of the townsfolk. And—and——"

Dave's voice trailed off.

"What's the matter?" Tom asked.

"Come toward me. Walk away from the wall. Now turn and look."

Tom turned . . . and was not encouraged by what he saw. A large waxy insect was crawling slowly along the wall. Behind its busy legs rose a thick, nasty-looking curved tail.

"Scorpion," Dave said. "Ugly beast."

"Is it poisonous? Can it kill?"

"I don't think its sting is fatal, but it sure won't do you any good. Now, how can we get him out of here without making him angry?"

"Swat him," Tom said.

Dave looked uneasy at that suggestion. Tom didn't like it much either. The scorpion was plump and big, and crushing it would be messy. But they couldn't let it crawl around the hut, a deadly threat to all.

They stood staring at the scorpion in bewilderment, neither of them knowing what to do. There was a long moment of silence, broken by the pleasant sound of a female voice asking a question in Swedish-tinged English.

"May I come in? It is Ursula."

"You'd better not," Dave said. "We've got a scorpion in here and we don't know what to do with it. Will you get us some help?"

Ursula laughed. The big blonde girl strode into the room and asked, "Where is it?"

"On the wall there," Tom said.

She smiled and walked toward the scorpion. She was wearing thick-soled, heavy boots, and Tom watched in astonishment as she deftly flicked the scorpion from the wall with the tip of one boot, and brought her foot down on it hard. There was a crunching sound.

"Scorpions cannot harm you so long as you see them first," she said easily. "I do not advise walking barefoot. The scorpions are very active at this time of year." Then she went on, as if unaware she had startled Tom and Dave. "I have come to tell you, we eat at six tonight. Do you eat meat? We are eating lamb tonight, in your honor. We eat lamb every other night too. But tonight it is in your honor."

Tom and his uncle exchanged glances. "Lamb sounds fine," Dave said.

"Good. I see you at dinner, then."

Ursula went out. Tom looked at the wreckage of the scorpion. "That girl's pretty tough," he said. "We were

71

standing here like scaredy-cats, and she just walked over and whomped it, as if it were an ant."

He began to laugh. He could see now why Kees had found his question about the girls' cooking abilities so funny. Ursula might be female, but she could match any male for toughness. Tom wondered how many girls back home would have dealt with the scorpion so briskly. Not many, he thought. Not many at all.

Dinner consisted of roast lamb and spiced barley, accompanied by soup and thick native bread. The cook for the evening had been Holger Carlson, and he, evidently, was famous for his fondness for spices. He took some good-natured joking about it.

The ten members of the expedition and their two guests ate together in one of the huts. A wire had been strung overhead, from which a couple of light bulbs dangled. A small whining generator provided power. "There's no electricity in the village," Ted Clay explained, "so we brought our own."

English was the official language of the expedition. Four of the ten were Americans, and some of them did not speak German, which was the second most widely used language in the group. Kees, Ursula, and Holger, who came from relatively small countries, seemed equally at home in English and German and appeared to know other languages too. Kees, in particular, was a versatile linguist; in addition to Dutch, English, and German, he admitted a knowledge of Nubian, Arabic, French and other modern languages, plus the ancient Egyptian language.

Tom was impressed by the casual way these people seemed to pick up languages. Mahmoud Hassan, the guide at

Akhnaten's city, had also been the master of a great many tongues. How did they do it? Tom wondered.

"It is not hard," Kees said, helping himself to a fat chunk of lamb. "You must develop the skill when you are young. I was born speaking Dutch, of course. Then I had to learn German, because——" his eyes were lowered for a moment "—because when I was a child my country was occupied by enemies, and we had to understand what they were saying. When I went to school, we had to study a foreign language. I chose English. So, by the time I was seven years old, I could speak three languages. The others came easily enough."

"It was almost the same with us," said Ursula. "In Sweden, most children study English in school. And we know German since we are so close to Germany. We pick up Norwegian and Danish readily because they are very much like Swedish. If we live in certain eastern parts of Sweden, we may learn Finnish too, and perhaps Russian. Then at university there comes Latin or Greek, and sometimes other languages."

Helmut asked, "What about you, Tom? Can you speak any language except English?"

Tom felt his cheeks glowing. "Well, I've studied some Spanish at school——"

Dr. Falke, who had been silently devouring his meat during this conversation, came to life. He turned to Tom and rattled off five or six sentences in high-speed Spanish. Tom could catch only a word or two.

He shook his head. "*No le entiendo muy bien,*" he said haltingly. "I don't understand you very well."

Dr. Falke's thick eyebrows lifted. More slowly, but still in Spanish, he said, "*Hablo muy de prisa?* I speak too fast?"

73

"I've only studied Spanish since last year," Tom confessed. "Where I live, we don't begin to learn foreign languages until we get to high school."

"That's the trouble," Janet Barker said with sudden vigor. "I've had the same problem, and Ted too, and Roy. In America, they don't teach us anything but English until we're in our teens. We don't get the knack of speaking other languages. Kees could speak three languages when he was seven, and now he can learn a new language in a couple of months. While we have to sweat and struggle to pick up what we need to know."

Ursula said, "And you, Dave? Are you also limited to English?"

"I learned a little Arabic this winter," Dave said. "For self-protection. I know some German, and I can bungle my way through French. That's about it."

"It is a great mistake," Dr. Falke muttered. "Every child should learn many languages. It develops the brain. Better: it teaches that there are different ways of considering the same idea. Maybe that is what is wrong with you Americans. You do not know enough languages, and so you are——"

"No politics, Ludwig!" came quickly from Dr. Decker, the other German professor. "You promised, now!"

Dr. Falke grinned abashedly. "You are right. I spoke foolishly. Pass me the meat! Enough talk!"

After dinner, Tom strolled outside for a look at his surroundings. Twilight was falling slowly. This close to the equator, the days were always long. The red disk of the sun gleamed in the west, cut in half by the mountains that rose on the far bank of the river. A hum of conversation came from the village. Little knots of villagers had gathered by their

74

houses, peering at the archaeologists as though they were men from Mars. Village boys splashed in the Nile; some were taking an evening dip; others were sailing toy boats.

Then the sun disappeared behind the western hills. With tropical suddenness, night descended. The twilight gray gave way to awesome black. The moon rode up in the sky, making the wide bosom of the river shine like polished silver. And, as if by the throwing of a switch, the stars began to blaze. A cool breeze from the north swept through the village, making the fronds of the tall palms sway. A man began to sing, far away. It was a high-pitched, droning song, and someone began to accompany it on a thin-voiced musical instrument.

The archaeologists were sitting quietly just within the front wall of one of the huts. Only the administration hut and one other had electricity; elsewhere, it was dark. Ursula sat by a table with a pile of broken pottery before her, most of the pieces less than an inch across. She was taking notes, and her pen scratched on busily. Dr. Falke was studying the aerial photographs again. Holger and Helmut were playing cards; Tom drifted over and watched, but was unable to follow the game.

"We invented it ourselves," Helmut told him after a while. "We call it Nubian rummy. The rules change every night."

Dave was pecking away at his typewriter. Kees was poring over long yellow sheets which bore penciled copies of hieroglyphic inscriptions. That was Kees' specialty, Tom had learned. He was an epigrapher whose task it was to copy and interpret the inscriptions the expedition discovered.

It was still early in the evening when the archaeologists began to drift away to bed.

"We go to sleep early here," Roy Fulton said. "It's hard

75

to do much in the evening because of the electricity problem. The sun's up in the small hours, and so are we. We do our best work between six and nine in the morning. After that it starts getting too hot."

It was only nine in the evening, and Tom didn't feel particularly sleepy. But soon there was no one left in the hut except Dave and Kees and himself, and Kees didn't look as though he wanted to be disturbed. Dave finished his writing and closed up the typewriter.

"Shall we call it a day?" Dave asked.

"Might as well," Tom agreed.

Morning sunlight flooded into their hut. Tom yawned, stretched, untangled himself from his light blanket, and got up from his cot. Dave was awake already. A quick face-splashing at the basin and Tom felt ready to begin his first day with the expedition. It was five-thirty in the morning. By six, work was getting under way.

The archaeologists were currently excavating the ruins of a building which lay at the edge of the sand dunes, a few hundred yards inland from the village. As they walked to the site, Kees explained what it was.

"This town seems to have been a trading post during the middle of the Eighteenth Dynasty. We've uncovered what appears to be the headquarters of the merchants."

"Eighteenth Dynasty—that was Akhnaten's dynasty, wasn't it?" Tom asked.

"Yes," Kees said. "But what we have here is earlier than Akhnaten. The trading post was set up during the reign of Amenhotep II. Say, 1440 B.C. He was Akhnaten's great-grandfather. A very unpleasant pharaoh, too. Quite bloodthirsty.

76

We think the merchants abandoned this place about the time Akhnaten came to the throne, possibly a little later."

"How can you tell?"

"There are many ways," Kees said. "The simplest is to look for inscriptions with Egyptian dates on them. We've known how to translate Egyptian hieroglyphics for more than a hundred and fifty years. And we've worked out a system of dating by comparing records, counting backward from fixed points like the date of an eclipse, and so forth. So, if we dig up a slab of stone that's dated 'Year Three of Amenhotep II,' we know where we are in time."

"And if there aren't any inscriptions?"

Kees smiled. "We look for other clues. The pottery style, for instance. Egyptologists have arrived at a knowledge of when certain styles of decorating pottery were popular. So if we find pottery of a particular style, it tells us how old the site is. It is a kind of detective work, you see. But not really terribly difficult, once you get the knack of it."

"Like learning foreign languages," said Tom.

"Yes. Exactly. We learn to read the language of time."

They were now at the site. It did not look very exciting. An area of the ground some twenty feet by twenty feet had been cleared of sand. A flimsy fence of wooden slats held together by wire had been set up to keep the sand from blowing back into the excavation. A nearby tent held the equipment of the archaeologists.

Tom walked to the edge of the excavated area. He saw a border of bricks outlining the square shape of the ancient trading post. At one point, the brick wall was about a dozen bricks high above the surrounding sand. At another, only a

77

single layer of bricks could be seen, while on the far side there was no trace of a wall at all.

Within the wall, the archaeologists had removed some of the sand. They had done it in terraces, it seemed. The sand had grown hard from being tightly packed, and they had cut it away in steplike blocks. One part of the excavation was six or seven feet deep. In another place, the sand had been cut away to a depth of only a foot.

Everyone was busy. Roy and Janet were on their knees in the middle of the site, scraping away with knives. They were removing the sand literally inch by inch. Big Holger Carlson, his heavy-featured face knotted in concentration, was crawling along the far side of the site, unrolling a tape measure and checking his findings against a sheet of paper he carried. Ursula was at the deepest part of the excavation, chipping at the hard-packed sand with an instrument which looked like a surgeon's scalpel. Helmut Blum, the photographer, was focusing on a group of small objects lying just within the left-hand wall, while Dr. Falke carefully placed a numbered tag next to each object before the picture was snapped.

Kees said, "There's the trading post, or all that's left of it. The merchants occupied it for some seventy years, we think. Then they pulled out and a native family moved in and lived in the building. They were pretty sloppy types, and let the roof collapse. The building was abandoned for five or ten years, and then another family moved in. They were driven away by Egyptian soldiers who used this as a barracks for about a dozen years. Then they went away. Local tribesmen pulled the brick walls of the building down and used the brick themselves. Sand covered everything for the next three thousand three hundred years."

78

Tom's eyes widened. He looked in bewilderment at the sand-filled ruin, then at the tall, freckled Dutch archaeologist. "How can you possibly know all that?" he asked.

Kees stroked his chin thoughtfully. "By keeping our eyes open," he said. "We are good detectives."

"But—to tell that the roof caved in, that one family left and another one took over—you'd need a crystal ball for that!" Tom objected.

"When you have watched us a few days, you will see how it is done," Kees said. "We take the sand off, inch by inch. Then we examine what it contains. The top few feet of sand contain nothing—meaning no one lived here for thousands of years. Then we find signs that soldiers lived here, soldiers whose equipment was of a type used in the Eighteenth Dynasty. We find broken daggers, we find spear points and sometimes handles, ornaments, an inscription or two. Luckily for us, people were not so neat in the ancient world as they are today. When something broke, they dropped it on the floor and it got covered by debris. We merely need to dig down to find it."

"And below the soldiers' things?" Tom asked.

"Pottery jugs—smashed, of course, but we can identify them. Children's toys. All the marks of a family that lived here. Below the family relics, a layer of sand more than a foot deep, containing nothing—telling us that the roof was off for a few years and sand blew in. Below the sand, more family goods, but a different, poorer family with cruder possessions. And then, down to the foundations. We have signs that merchants lived here first. Everything is nicely preserved for us, even their account books."

"I begin to see," Tom said. He looked toward Dave, who was standing by, smiling fascinatedly.

Kees beckoned. "Come around this way. See how we work? We do one layer at a time. But first we dig a trial trench, down to the bottom, so we know what the entire site is likely to contain. Then we work down, layer by layer. Whatever we find, we number and photograph so we know afterward which layer we found it in. Meanwhile Holger is doing a ground plan of the building. I examine any inscriptions that turn up. Each of us has his job. Ursula studies the pottery, and——"

"Kees! Kees, will you come here a moment?"

It was Janet calling. Kees excused himself, stepped over the ruined wall of the old building, and went to her side. She pointed into the excavation. Kees knelt and peered at something she was showing him. He seemed to forget all about Tom and Dave. A moment later, he was scribbling notes on a pad.

Standing just outside the work area, Tom and Dave watched the archaeologists at their labors. It was silent here, with the stillness of a library or a church. Each member of the team had his own work to do, and he went about it with quiet efficiency.

Tom said, "I guess I never realized that archaeologists worked like this. I thought they just stuck a spade in the ground and dug up museum pieces."

"No true archaeologist works like that, Tom. It hasn't been that way for a hundred years. They're looking for knowledge, not for museum pieces. A piece of pottery can be more useful to them than a gold statue."

"Look at them, though. Peeling the sand away the way

you'd peel the skin off an onion! How can they be so patient? If I were doing it, I'd want to shovel all the sand away at once to find out what was down below."

"But then you wouldn't know who had lived here and in what order," Dave said. "You'd jumble up all the different layers. You wouldn't get a fraction of the information they've been getting."

"That's true enough. I guess that's why they're archaeologists and I'm not. I'd never have the patience to sift through all those pieces of pottery."

"You learn patience."

"The way you learn to speak foreign languages, I suppose," Tom said.

He looked down into the excavation again. It was fascinating to watch the archaeologists at work. And yet——

"Dave?"

"Mmm?"

"I don't want to sound like a dope," Tom said. "But there's one thing troubling me about all this."

"Which is?"

"It's very interesting to watch the way they work, the technique and all. But it what they're doing going to be interesting to anybody but another archaeologist? I mean, I admire them for being able to dig into an ancient ruined brick house and find out who lived there and how long—but does anyone really care about that?"

"They care," Dave said.

"But they won't discover anything earthshaking down there, will they? When they're all through, they'll know a little more about trading posts of the Eighteenth Dynasty, whatever good that'll be. I guess it'll all form part of the big picture of what Egypt was like. But——" Tom kicked at the sand. "What I'm getting at is this, Dave. You came here to write magazine articles and later a book. You're not going to be writing for an audience of archaeologists. Are most people going to care a hoot about an Eighteenth Dynasty trading post?"

"Probably not," Dave admitted. "But they've got other projects to deal with here. Maybe something newsworthy will turn up."

"And if not?"

"I'll manage," Dave said. "When I came out here, I knew the odds were against anything spectacular being found. I intend to tell the day-by-day story of archaeology in Nubia, the sweat and toil, the monotonous sifting of sand. And if anything big turns up, well, that'll just be a big bonus for everyone."

Tom hoped Dave was right. Somehow he doubted that work of this sort was going to set magazine readers on fire, no matter how interesting it seemed to someone right on the spot. For Dave's sake, he hoped a bigger discovery would be made. For his own, too.

If only Sheikh Ibrahim would come back!

Tom had talked himself into believing that wonders were hidden in that puzzling passageway. He knew he was letting himself in for a big disappointment if the underground tunnel didn't reveal something extraordinary. But he couldn't help daydreaming about the things it might contain.

Otherwise, he thought, it was going to be a long, hot summer for him, watching the ten archaeologists sifting through sand for bits and pieces of the dead past.

CHAPTER SEVEN

THE SHEIKH RETURNS

Much to Tom's relief, he didn't have to spend his morning standing around watching the members of the expedition work. Dr. Falke called him into the excavation and gave him a task.

He was assigned the job of helping to remove sand from the side of the building that hadn't been excavated deeply yet. It was not very taxing work. On many expeditions, Dave told him, that sort of labor was entrusted to natives. It did not mean any responsibilities for Tom, other than to be careful as he dug. "If you uncover anything—anything at all," Dr. Falke cautioned him, "stop digging at once, Thomas. Call another member of the expedition. Do not lift an object from its place, no matter how trivial it seems."

Tom dug away. It was something to do, at least, and made him feel as though he were part of the expedition. Delicately he slipped his small spade into the sand, scooped up a spadeful, sifted through it, dumped it into the wheelbarrow, and dug again. He eyed the sand closely, as though he expected to find it full of gold coins. But there was nothing there, not so much as a bit of shattered pottery. Where he was working,

83

the archaeological material lay several feet down, covered by wind-blown desert sand.

By nine in the morning, the sun was high in the sky and the heat was beginning to be unpleasant. The archaeologists had been at work for three hours, saying little as they dug and probed and measured and photographed and sketched.

Then Dr. Falke said, "We stop for a while now."

The hot part of the day was beginning. It was back to the village for everyone. Both the girls and some of the men got into bathing suits and went running down to the Nile for a dip. Tom joined them. The water, which looked so brown and muddy from the deck of a boat, seemed blue and clear at close range. Getting into the river was like getting into a luke-warm bath, although the water was cool compared to the air. Tom swam out a good distance from shore. After the long morning of patient work, it was good to get some vigorous exercise.

He wondered about the crocodiles. Who knew what might be moving slowly through the depths below him? No one else seemed to be worried—but he paddled rapidly back to shore, all the same, and stayed close to the others afterward.

There were many Nubian children at the river's edge. The young ones wore nothing at all; the older ones were dressed in flowing, spotless gowns, white or striped. None came near the archaeologists, though they all stared at them.

"Aren't they ever friendly?" Tom asked. "Don't they do anything but stare?"

"Not while Sheikh Ibrahim's away," Roy Fulton said. "He's just about the only one in the village who speaks anything but Nubian. Some of the women know a little Arabic, but not much. Since they can't communicate with us, they're nervous. They're a shy bunch."

"Is Sheikh Ibrahim friendly?"

"Oh, yes. He's a grand sort. He and his son. They're not like the others. They've traveled a lot, at least by local standards. They aren't shy at all. But when the Sheikh's away, the rest keep their distance."

After swim time it was back to work for the archaeologists —not in the open under the blazing sun, but in the coolness of their mud huts. It was time to write up the results of the morning's work. Everyone kept a logbook, setting down in minute detail everything that he did at the site. Thus, it would be possible later to reconstruct step by step the entire process of the excavation.

It was absolutely necessary to work that way, Tom was told. All excavation was a process of destruction. The ruined trading post would be dug down to its foundations, and when the archaeologists were finished, nothing would remain. So it was vital to make a layer-by-layer account of the work, with many sketches and photographs to show where everything had been. Other archaeologists could then study the reports and form as clear an idea of what the trading post had been like as if they had done the excavating themselves. In the early days of archaeology, in the nineteenth century, things had not been done that carefully.

"Some of the old boys were dynamic and persistent and hard workers," Ted Clay said, "but it's too bad that they discovered so much. They ruined many things they touched. If only a few of the choice sites hadn't been discovered for another fifty years——"

"But without the mistakes of the pioneers," Janet said,

"modern archaeology would never have developed. Someone had to begin."

Ted shrugged. "Why couldn't they have done their pioneering at less important places, then? When you think of all that was botched up because they didn't understand how to dig, because they didn't make records properly, because they mixed up the strata, because they didn't know how to preserve what they dug up, because——"

"There is still much waiting to be discovered," Dr. Falke said quietly. "Let us hope that archaeologists a hundred years from now will not criticize *our* technique so bitterly, eh?"

So two hours were occupied by entering records of the morning's work. Then it was noon, and time for lunch—a light meal of fruit and vegetables washed down with goat's milk. Holger sighed and told Tom how much he would like a good cold bottle of Danish beer. But Nubia was a Moslem land, and all alcoholic beverages were forbidden. No wine, no beer, no liquor—but all the goat's milk anybody cared to drink.

Siesta time followed. The heat was incredible, now. It usually reached 120° in the shade at midday, and nobody cared to measure the temperature in the sun. All village activities were halted. Silence reigned. No one went out of his hut. The archaeologists relaxed, reading, napping, playing cards. Helmut sat before the short-wave radio that was their chief contact with the outside world and tried to tune in news broadcasts. From time to time, he looked back over his shoulder and offered a bulletin:

"The President of the United States has gone to visit Berlin," he reported. "There has been an earthquake in Burma. The Russians have sent up a new space platform."

86

No one seemed to be paying attention. To Tom, the outside world seemed terribly far away now. All the world conflicts that loomed so big in the newspapers back home seemed unimportant. The rockets being built for exploration of the moon, the debates in Congress and the United Nations, the squabbles of rival nations—all were unreal and misty now.

What was real?

The sun was real, burning in the Nubian sky as it burned three hundred sixty-five days a year. The desert was real. The mountains were real. The Nile, flowing placidly toward the sea, was real. Nubia was a changeless world, Tom thought, where all was as it had been in the days of the pharaohs.

No, he told himself. No, that was not so.

The modern world had reached even into timeless Nubia. The great dam at Aswan, hundreds of miles to the north, would have its effects down here in another year or two. This entire village, lying so close to the edge of the Nile, would be flooded. Even the old trading post, inland a fair distance, would disappear, for the shore was flat here and the creeping water would inundate everything. These gaily decorated mud huts would sag and dissolve. The handsome palm trees lining the shore would be swallowed up right to their crowns. The people of the village, driven from their ancestral lands, would trek southward into Upper Nubia, taking up new dwellings in strange places.

This part of the world seemed an island in time, cut off from the twentieth century. But it was not so at all, Tom thought. Not at all.

In midafternoon, when the heat had relented a little, the archaeologists returned to their trading post site for a few additional hours of excavation. Then, about five, the working day came to a halt. Six o'clock was dinnertime; the cook for that night was Kees, who did his best to make the lamb and vegetables taste different from the lamb and vegetables of all the other nights. After dinner, it was time to record the results of the afternoon's digging. A couple of hours of relaxation and conversation followed, and then to bed.

As the group began to break up, Holger Carlson stopped Tom and asked, "Do you wish to do a little sight-seeing tomorrow?"

"Where?"

"Delgo. There is a temple there you might care to see. I have no work to do here tomorrow, and I thought I would go to sketch the temple at Delgo. Would you join me?"

"I'd be glad to," Tom said. He looked at his uncle. "Dave? Will you come too?"

"I don't think so, thanks. I'd like to stay here and observe the work. You and Holger go. You can tell me about it when you get back."

"We will leave immediately after breakfast," Holger said. "It would not be good to get there too close to the middle of the day."

Tom didn't need an alarm clock to wake him the next morning. As on the day before, the bright sunlight took care of the job. Holger had the jeep ready, and he had packed a lunchbox for them.

The big Dane drove through the village and left it at the southern end. The road disappeared and they jounced along the plain of the river. Soon they were at Delgo again. Holger left the jeep in the middle of the town, put his sketchbook under his arm, and handed Tom the lunchbox.

"We hire a boat now," he said. "The temple is on the other shore."

Some quick haggling in sign language got them a boatman. The broad sail of their boat bellied out as they crossed the wide river. The boatman moored his craft and settled down on the rocky shore, closing his eyes and slipping almost at once into an easy doze.

"Is he going to wait for us?" Tom asked.

"That is right."

"But we're going to be here all morning!"

Holger smiled and said softly, "He has nothing better to do. The small amount I gave him buys his services for the whole day. We cannot very well swim back, you know."

They left the boatman by the shore, and began to scramble up the rocks toward the temple. Holger moved with fantastic agility, considering that he was a big man, weighing well over two hundred pounds. Tom, more cautious, stayed behind him, not wanting to risk a twisted ankle or a broken leg. In a few minutes he was panting badly, and Holger stopped to wait for him.

"I am going too fast?"

"No," Tom said without much conviction. "I can keep up."

"When I am not doing archaeological research," said Holger, "I climb mountains. It is agreeable exercise. Last January, I climbed in the Swiss Alps. Do you climb?"

"Not really," Tom said. "At least, I haven't done any yet. There aren't any real mountains near where I live."

Holger chuckled. "Do you think Denmark has mountains? The Copenhagen Alps, eh? I come from a flat land. I look for the mountains in other lands. Next year, I will be in the

89

United States. I will study in California. I will climb Mount Rainier, I think."

"That's in Washington, not in California."

"It is nearby, though. A few hundred miles. I will spend a weekend. You have seen Mount Rainier? Is it not beautiful?"

"I've seen pictures," Tom said. "I've never been to the Northwest."

Holger looked at him strangely. "Your own country and you have not seen it all? When I was your age, I knew Denmark like the back of my hand."

"I can see you've never been to the United States, Holger. It's a big place. You could put all of Denmark down in it and never find it again. It would take you a long time to see my whole country."

"Perhaps. Perhaps. Anyway, I climb Mount Rainier. Maybe you come with me, eh? We climb it together. You look like a climber. You have big shoulders, strong legs. We will go, yes? And your uncle, too. The three of us, right to the summit."

The word "summit" brought them to the top of the heap of rocks up which they had been scrambling for several minutes. Holger pointed ahead.

"There is the temple," he said.

The building had come upon hard times, Tom saw. Possibly it had been an impressive temple once, but only three columns were still standing; the rest of it had tumbled down and shattered.

They stepped onto the temple platform. Picking their way around the fallen debris, they approached the three columns, which were covered with hieroglyphic inscriptions. The carvings had been chiseled with the sharpness of line and beauty of design which marked all the Egyptian inscriptions Tom had seen. But there was something odd about these columns. It seemed as though other inscriptions lay below the ones on top—as if the builders had smeared a layer of stucco over earlier carvings to hide them.

And—what was this——?

On all three columns, Tom saw what seemed to be the image of the disk of the sun, cut deep, with rays emanating outward. The words of the inscription ran right across the solar disk, but did not completely hide it. Tom had seen disks like that before—in the murals of Akhnaten's city!

"Look," he said, pointing at the nearest column. "That circle there, under the hieroglyphics. Isn't that Akhnaten's symbol for Aten?"

Holger nodded casually. He seemed not at all impressed by Tom's knowledge of Egyptology—nor by the presence of the symbol on the columns.

"Yes," he said. "Yes, that is Akhnaten's doing. He built this temple, you know."

Tom felt a shiver of awe. Once again the rebel pharaoh!

"Here?" he asked. "I didn't know he had built anything this far south."

"Oh, yes," Holger said. "Nubia was very sympathetic toward Akhnaten's religious movement. This is thought to be the temple of Gem-Aten. It is the only known Aten temple in Nubia. Come look at this, though."

Tom was bubbling with more questions about Akhnaten, but Holger had already walked away. Willy-nilly, Tom followed him. Holger pointed to odd openings in the rear wall of the temple platform.

"What are they?" Tom asked.

"Drains. To let the rain water out. Very significant. Very interesting."

"Rain water?" Tom repeated, confused. "I thought it never rained here. Well, hardly ever."

Holger nodded. "You are right. Rain is a rarity in Nubia today. So these drains tell us a great deal. Obviously, the climate was different here when the temple was built, yes? It is a stone temple, not brick, and it has drains for the run-off of water. This helps us to understand certain tribute records of Nubia which talk of the land's great fertility. Nubia is not fertile now. But it seems it once had much more rain so it did not depend altogether on the Nile for water. One fact dovetails with the next. That is how we learn."

Tom had to admit that it was an interesting observation. Once again, he had been shown how the archaeologists patiently added clue to clue in order to assemble their picture of the far past.

Yet he was not able to get as excited over these drains as Holger, the specialist in ancient architecture, did. What caught Tom's imagination was not so much the design of the temple as the hopes and dreams of the man who had built it.

He asked, "Who covered over Akhnaten's inscriptions? Was it done by Horemheb?"

"No," Holger answered. "These inscriptions have been studied, and they were carved in the time of Seti I. He is Nineteenth Dynasty—the second pharaoh after Horemheb. He ruled about fifty years after Akhnaten died."

"No one covered over Akhnaten's inscriptions for fifty years down here? I thought that his enemies went to work on all his temples right after he died."

"It took many years," said Holger. "The real persecution

of the Aten religion did not start until Horemheb became pharaoh. That was long after Akhnaten's death. No doubt this temple was forgotten for a while. We are five hundred miles from Thebes, and no one bothered to do anything to Akhnaten's words here until Seti's time. Look. Look here."

He indicated a figure carved on the column.

"This represents the god Amon," Holger said. "The god whom Akhnaten tried to destroy. And here, beneath the image—can you see?"

Tom looked closely. The outlines of Amon seemed to cover another figure. Rough chisel marks showed how the earlier figure had been hacked away before Amon's image had been carved. Stepping back a few feet, Tom took another look, and, suddenly, the underimage became clear. The long head, the jutting jaw, the strangely shaped legs—there could be no doubt of it. Akhnaten himself had once been represented here, before the destroyers came!

Tom and Holger spent a quiet morning. Holger sketched the temple, measuring its dimensions and quickly reducing them to a diagram on paper. Tom prowled around, searching for other pictures of Akhnaten and his family. It was hard to be certain of anything; a few blurred lines only hinted at the drawings which had once been there. It was strange to have encountered Akhnaten again, here in the heart of Nubia. Tom had not thought about the sad-eyed pharaoh for many days.

Aten had been worshipped here as well as in Egypt, then. And, since news must have traveled slowly in the old days, perhaps it had been many years before word of Akhnaten's death had reached Nubia. Maybe, Tom thought, the Nubian priests of Aten had gone on celebrating the rites of their religion, paying homage to the One God, Aten, long after cruel Amon had re-established his power in distant Thebes. Until one day the emissaries of Pharaoh Seti came, and declared that Aten was to be honored no longer, and cut the dead monarch's inscriptions from the columns of his monuments.

When the sun had climbed high in the sky, they had their lunch and started back. Holger awakened the dozing boatman, and they made the slow journey across the Nile to Delgo. They found the jeep surrounded by a crowd of curious Nubians who melted silently away the moment Tom and Holger approached.

"There is another good temple to see not far from here," Holger said, as they jolted back toward their own village. "It is at Sulb—a temple of Amenhotep III, Akhnaten's father. I have seen it, and ever since I have wanted to draw it. Perhaps we will go there tomorrow if there is still no work for me to do here, yes?"

"I'd like to very much," Tom said.

But as the jeep pulled into the village, it was clear that something unusual had happened—something that would change their plans for the next day. It was nearly noon, but the villagers had not settled into their midday siesta. They were clustered in an excited group in front of a hut. Tom saw several of the archaeologists in the circle too—Dr. Falke, Kees van Vlaardingen, and two others who were barely visible in the crowd.

Tom and Holger left the jeep and went forward.

"What's happening?" Tom asked.

Kees swung around, grinning broadly. "Sheikh Ibrahim is back! He returned on the morning boat!"

CHAPTER EIGHT

DOWN INTO DARKNESS

Tom had expected Sheikh Ibrahim to be venerable and wizened, with a long white beard. Bearded he was, but the beard was black with streaks of gray. The Sheikh was a man about forty, powerfully built, his skin black as night, his eyes gleaming and intelligent. He was dressed in a flowing white robe and wore a white cap.

Dr. Falke managed to get the Sheikh away from the mob of admiring villagers and over to the huts where the archaeologists were staying. A boy walked at the Sheikh's side. "His son," Holger explained. "Ali Hosein."

Ali Hosein appeared to be about twelve or thirteen. He was a head shorter than Tom, lean and wiry. His skin was dark like his father's; his features were sharp; his expression alert and keen. Tom got the impression that there was tremendous strength packed away in the boy's slender body— that, if he had to, Ali Hosein could run for miles or swim back and forth across the Nile for hours without growing tired. There was not an ounce of spare flesh on him.

In the administration hut, Dr. Falke introduced Tom and Dave to the Sheikh and his son. Sheikh Ibrahim held out his hand gravely, first to Dave, then to Tom.

95

"Welcome to our village," he said, speaking English with a British accent. "I hope you will find yours a useful visit and a pleasant one. We are happy to offer our hospitality—poor though it is." The Sheikh smiled. "I present my son, Ali Hosein."

The boy stepped forward. His eyes flashed from Tom to Dave, back to Tom. Then he grinned. "Hello," he said. "Are you Americans?"

"That's right," Tom said.

"George Washington. Ike Eisenhower. John Kennedy. See? I know Americans! You like it here?"

"Very much."

"But it's hot. Very hot! Yes? Not this hot in America?"

"Not where I come from," Tom said. "There are deserts in the Southwest where it gets almost this hot. But I'm from the East."

Ali Hosein frowned thoughtfully. "Southwest—East—not so easy to understand. Come outside and show me."

He led Tom from the hut. Dr. Falke and Sheikh Ibrahim were busily conferring and did not seem to want company. There were villagers wandering around outside, but they cleared away as Ali Hosein and Tom walked through their midst toward the river.

"Now," Ali Hosein said, "this way, south; this way, north. Which is east and which is west?"

Tom understood the problem. To a Nubian villager—to anyone who dwelt along the Nile—the only directions which mattered were north and south. No one ever went very far from the river in an easterly or westerly direction. The two banks of the Nile needed no identification other than "our side of the river" and "the other side of the river."

Tom pointed toward the mountains. "West," he said. "America's that way. And this way—toward the desert— that's east."

Ali Hosein closed his eyes a moment, absorbing the information. "Very good," he said. "East, west. How many children do you have?"

The abrupt change of subject caught Tom completely off guard. "What?"

"Children. I say it right? How many children? *Les enfants?*"

"I don't have any children," Tom said, laughing. "I'm not even married. I'm only fifteen years old. I go to high school."

"Fifteen? Is old not to be married. I get married next year, maybe. If lucky, I have a son when I your age."

"How old are you now?"

"Thirteen," Ali Hosein said. He flashed a glittering grin. "My father, he was married when thirteen. I am his seventh son. The others don't live here any more. One in Cairo, one in Alexandria, one in Khartoum. One goes to school in Addis Ababa. You have been there? In Ethiopia. South. My oldest brother, Ahmad Ibrahim, he is in Moscow, Russia. The Russians are teaching him to be a doctor. They want to teach him to be a Communist, too, but I don't think he learns that. He says Russia is a very cold place. Some day, I go to United States for a visit. I think I go where you say it is hot. Southwest."

Tom was finding it hard to keep up with the Nubian boy's torrent of words. It was amazing enough that Ali Hosein should speak English this well—but his lightning leaps from one subject to another left Tom a little dazzled.

97

"Where did you learn such good English?" Tom asked, trying to slow down the conversation.

"Cairo," Ali Hosein said. "I lived in Cairo five years. They teach me English and French there. I speak four languages, English, French, Arabic, and our own language. My father speaks those languages, too. We talk to each other in English so we don't forget how. What languages do you speak?"

Tom felt color flooding into his cheeks. It seemed that wherever he went on this trip, he ran into linguists. "English," he said, shamefaced. "And a little Spanish. I'm not very good at languages, I guess."

"You play baseball?" Ali Hosein asked.

They were off again on a new track. "Yes, sure," Tom said. "I play a lot of ball back home. Outfield, usually."

"Here there is no room for baseball. In Cairo, I watched United States soldiers playing. They let me play, but I never hit the ball. I played cricket, too. I liked baseball better. In cricket, you stand still too much. Was President Kennedy a friend of yours?"

Tom was getting used to Ali Hosein's habit of changing the subject every few sentences. "A friend of mine? No, I never saw him—except on television."

"Very great man. My father cried the day he died. I still remember it. I wrote to him, once. I said, 'Come to Egypt, come to Nubia.' But he did not come. He——"

Tom heard voices behind him. The others were emerging from the meeting, now. He and Ali Hosein turned. Dr. Falke and Sheikh Ibrahim were both smiling.

Dave left the group and walked toward them. "It's all right," he said to Tom. "Sheikh Ibrahim has given his permission for the excavating of the passageway. He's going to explain things to the villagers now."

"What is this?" Ali Hosein asked.

Tom said, "While you and your father were away, the archaeologists discovered a tunnel that runs under the village. Your people wouldn't let anyone dig there until Sheikh Ibrahim came back."

Ali Hosein's eyes sparkled. "Is there gold there?"

"No one knows what's there," Tom said. "That's why the archaeologists want to explore it."

"They will find gold and treasure there," said Ali Hosein matter-of-factly. He glanced up at Dave. "You are the brother of Tom?" he asked.

"The uncle," Dave said. "The brother of his father."

"You look like brothers. How many children do you have, Uncle of Tom?"

Dave looked baffled. Tom chuckled. This was where he had come in.

"I'll be back in a little while," he said. Dave could talk with Ali Hosein for a while. Tom wanted a drink of water and some fresh clothes, for he had become covered with sand and dust during his journey to the temple at Delgo.

Talking to the Nubian boy was fun, Tom thought. But it was hard work, too. In a way, it was as strenuous as that scramble up the hill had been.

The new excavation was started early the next morning. Only part of the expedition group was involved. Holger Carlson, Kees van Vlaardingen, Dr. Marshall, and Dr. Falke worked on the passageway; the other six archaeologists were still out at the trading-post site, finishing digging there. It was not considered good technique to hop from one job to another without finishing what had been already begun.

Sheikh Ibrahim and Ali Hosein were on hand, too. And, of course, so were Tom and Dave. The entrance to the passageway was almost exactly in the center of the village. A thin layer of sand covered four large slabs of stone. Holger brushed the sand away, and Kees knelt down to examine the stone slabs.

For long minutes, Kees studied them, moving slowly from one to the next like a jeweler examining a gem for hidden flaws. Then he stood up, shaking his head. "No trace of an inscription. We can proceed."

Dr. Falke clicked off a photograph of the stones. Since Helmut Blum was busy taking photos at the other site, the bearded expedition leader was manning the camera. He stepped back, and Holger, grunting slightly, slipped a crowbar into the ground and pried one of the heavy slabs out of the way. A moment later, he lifted a second slab, and then the third, and the fourth.

A gaping hole lay open. Steps led down into darkness.

"Get the generator going," Dr. Falke said.

Kees began to turn the crank. Dr. Marshall, a pale, thin-faced man who was co-leader of the expedition, unpacked rolls of electrical wire. Dr. Falke and Kees, each carrying powerful flashlights, stepped downward into the opening.

"May we follow you?" Dave asked.

Dr. Falke smiled apologetically. "Not just yet, please. Until we know what is there——"

They vanished from sight. Tom walked to the edge of

the tunnel and peered in. He could see nothing at all, not even the flicker of their flashlights.

"They've gone around a bend in the tunnel," he said.

Holger scratched his chin. "Perhaps I should go after them," he said. "If the tunnel is not structurally sound, if it should collapse while they are in there——"

"I'll have the electric lights ready in a minute, Holger," Dr. Marshall said. "Don't go in until you can see where you're going."

Ali Hosein nudged Tom sharply in the ribs. "They will find gold," he insisted. "Much, much gold!"

"How do you know? Has anyone from the village been in there?"

"Never," Ali Hosein said. "But there is treasure there. I know. Much treasure!"

Tom heard footsteps. Then Dr. Falke and Kees emerged from the tunnel.

"The passage extends about twelve or fifteen feet," Dr. Falke said. "Kees didn't see any inscriptions. We ran into a stone wall as soon as we went round the bend."

"A *stone* wall?" Holger repeated. "Not simply sand?"

"Stone. Very carefully placed. Whoever built this tunnel didn't want anyone going deeper into it than that wall." Dr. Falke's voice was calm, but Tom sensed an underlying excitement in his tone. Dr. Falke, a veteran of years of archaeology, knew better than to jump to unfounded conclusions—but it seemed to Tom that the German archaeologist was definitely on edge now.

Sheikh Ibrahim asked, "If you remove the wall, is there danger that the tunnel will collapse?"

"I don't think so," said Dr. Falke. "Holger will check everything before we proceed. And we'll brace the tunnel roof as we dig. We have your permission to continue, do we not, Sheikh Ibrahim?"

The village leader smiled. "Of course," he said quietly. "You must find out what lies beyond the wall. Perhaps my son is right. Perhaps there is treasure there—golden treasure or the treasure of new knowledge. You must open the wall."

No one showed any sign of haste. Dr. Marshall brought the electrical generator to the mouth of the tunnel and then he strung lights along the passage. Holger went inside and spent half an hour prodding at the walls and roof of the tunnel to see how sturdy it was. Then he came out and entered the Nubian villager's house that lay just above the tunnel, making sure that no harm would come to anyone or anything in the house in case there was an unexpected collapse.

Ted Clay came over from the other site, carrying a load of wooden beams. He and Holger set to work reinforcing the roof of the tunnel. The passageway was about five feet high and nearly four feet wide. When at last they were ready to go to work on the stone barrier, Dr. Falke took some flashbulb photographs. Then he allowed Tom and Dave to look around the tunnel.

Ted and Holger ordered everyone else out so they could set to work. Standing in the broiling heat outside, Tom could hear the ring of crowbar and pick against stone. Every few minutes, Ted or Holger would appear at the entrance, carrying a heavy block of granite that had been pried loose. Tom, Dave, and Kees hauled the blocks to one side so they would not close up the entrance.

After what seemed like hours, Holger came out of the tunnel, stripped to the waist and streaming with perspiration. "The wall is half down," he reported. "We can see beyond it now."

"What do you see?" three people asked at once.

"Passages," Holger said. "Five, six of them. Leading in every direction."

"Very good," Dr. Falke said quietly. "We have found something, then. Something more than a mere cellar, I think. Kees, are there any inscriptions on those blocks of stone?"

"Nothing," Kees said. "They're absolutely blank. Whoever built that wall evidently didn't have time to decorate it."

"It was a rushed job," said Holger. "The workmanship is very poor. The blocks do not fit well together. The workers must have hurried indeed."

"I could climb through," Ali Hosein suggested. "I could go in the opening and find the treasure!"

Dr. Falke smiled. "We must all be patient," he said gently. "Whatever is in there has waited many years to be discovered. We must move step by step. Holger, do you wish to rest now, or to finish taking down the wall?"

"The wall," Holger said. "I rest later."

He went back into the tunnel, and soon the sound of pick and crowbar could be heard again. While the two men worked, Dr. Falke kept a wary eye on the ground above the tunnel, watching for the slightest sign of a cave-in. Tom noticed that Sheikh Ibrahim, too, was keeping a close watch. Both men seemed outwardly relaxed. Yet each was protecting his own—Dr. Falke guarding the safety of Holger and Ted, Sheikh Ibrahim worried about the property of the family whose house happened to be built above the old tunnel.

The tunnel seemed to go straight down for seven or eight feet before it went forward. There was plenty of solid ground between its roof and the mud hut above, and any weakness in structure would be checked by the bracing wooden beams.

After a while, Ted emerged. "The wall is down to its last row of blocks," he said. "We can step over them and go deeper. Do you want to come with us?"

Dr. Falke beckoned to Kees. Once again, they entered the tunnel. Dr. Falke paused and looked back over his shoulder. "Sheikh Ibrahim, would you care to join us?"

"Very well," the Sheikh said.

Ali Hosein plucked at the sleeve of his father's long white robe. But the Sheikh shook his head, making a quick flicking gesture with the tips of his fingers, as though brushing a troublesome mosquito away. Ali Hosein hung his head in disappointment as his father went down into the passage.

Tom turned to Dave. "Maybe we're on to something big after all? Something a little bigger than a trading post, at any rate."

"Maybe," Dave said tightly. "We'll see what we see."

"Treasure," said Ali Hosein. "Gold and silver. Precious jewels. One of the great ones lies buried there. I am sure of it! One of the very great!"

The minutes crawled by, lengthening into more than a quarter of an hour. The little knot of curious villagers lost interest in the proceedings and wandered away, leaving Tom, Dave, Ali Hosein, and Dr. Marshall clustered by the mouth of the tunnel. Noon had arrived, and the sunlight beat down unmercifully. Tom felt as though his brains were being baked in his white pith helmet. The whining drone of the electrical generator became a nuisance. A scorpion came over to investigate, lifted its venomous sting in a menacing gesture, then scuttered away into the sand.

What were they doing in there? Had the tunnel collapsed somewhere beyond the wall, trapping them all? Or had they stumbled across some fabulous treasure that held them spell-bound?

Suddenly, Sheikh Ibrahim reappeared. He was smiling in an odd way. Holger was with him.

The Sheikh said to Tom and Dave, "You are asked to go inside and look."

Ali Hosein stepped forward with them. Sheikh Ibrahim extended a hand quickly and caught his son by one shoulder. He spoke to him sharply. The words were Nubian, but it was not hard to guess his meaning. Ali Hosein's shoulders slumped unhappily.

Holger led Tom and Dave down into the tunnel.

The air was dry and musty. The electrical wiring had been strung along the passage with dim bulbs every twenty feet or so. There was an elbow-bend in the tunnel. They came to the place where the wall had been, and stepped over its foundation. Just beyond, the tunnel seemed to fork in many directions. Holger gestured toward the new passages.

"They seem like dead ends," he said. "But we will have to examine them all closely. Come this way."

They followed along the path of the electric lights. The tunnel twisted and turned, doubling back on itself so often that Tom lost all sense of direction. When they had gone what seemed like a hundred yards, there was another right-angle turn. Dr. Falke and Kees were just beyond it, peering intently at something.

Tom saw that a new stone wall blocked the tunnel here.

"Another dead end?" he asked.

"Something lies beyond," Dr. Falke said. He stepped away from the wall. "Look. Do these symbols mean anything to you?"

The granite blocks of the barrier bore carvings. They were hasty and crude, not nearly so elegant as the inscriptions Tom had seen elsewhere. Haphazard rows of hieroglyphics ran helter-skelter over the surface.

One symbol looked familiar. The sun-disk! The symbol of Aten!

Tom pointed to it. "This, here—the disk with the rays! It's Akhnaten's religious symbol, isn't it?"

"It is," Dr. Falke said. "And this——"

He indicated a group of hieroglyphics framed by an oval line. A cartouche, Tom knew; it contained a royal name. Within the oval was the figure of a bird, something that looked like the sun, and several other characters.

Dr. Falke's finger quivered as he pointed toward it.

"The cartouche of Akhnaten," he said in a low voice.

CHAPTER NINE

THE GOLDEN PHARAOH

The hubbub at the archaeologists' camp that night lasted well past the usual bedtime. Nearly everyone had a theory of his own. Only the three older men, Dr. Falke, Dr. Marshall, and Dr. Decker, sat back quietly, refusing to guess at what might lie behind the last wall they had encountered.

Holger was the loudest and most insistent of the theorists. "It may be a tomb," he said. "Akhnaten's tomb."

"That's fantastic!" Kees scoffed. "Akhnaten was never buried. His body was torn to pieces by the priests of Amon."

"How do you know?" Roy Fulton asked. "Where's the proof?"

"It's only logical," Kees said.

"Is it so logical?" demanded Holger. "There is no known inscription telling of Akhnaten's fate. We know that his religion had followers here in Nubia. We have all seen the temple at Delgo with the obliterated inscriptions of Akhnaten. What I say is this: that when he died, some of his followers smuggled his body out of Egypt and laid it to rest here, where his enemies couldn't find it and destroy it."

Kees snorted. "Very imaginative! You should write novels instead of being an archaeologist, Holger!"

The big Dane made a face at Kees. Everyone laughed.

One thought had been circling round and round in Tom's mind all afternoon. He could not forget the weird way that Ali Hosein had said, without a trace of doubt, "There is treasure there." Could it be?

Tom said, "Let's assume it *is* Akhnaten's tomb. Would it be as splendid as Tutankhamen's? Would it have all the works of art and golden treasure that his tomb did?"

"Not very likely," Helmut said. "If Holger's idea is correct, Akhnaten was buried quickly and secretly. There was little time to collect much treasure for his tomb."

"The inscriptions on the wall are hastily done," Kees observed. "The wall itself was a poor job. Helmut is right: the tomb, if it is a tomb, cannot hold anything very splendid. Some local chieftain, perhaps, put away quickly and carelessly."

"If it's really Akhnaten's tomb," said Ted Clay, "it wouldn't matter at all if it had a scrap of gold in it. The historical importance is what would count, not the value of the antiquities. We'd have answered one of the big problems in Egyptology, by finding out where Akhnaten was buried."

Helmut nodded vigorously. "As for me, I hope there is not a bit of valuable treasure behind that wall!"

"Why?" Janet asked. "So you'll have fewer pictures to take?"

Helmut did not look amused. "It is not that at all. We will have our hands full if the tomb contains gold or silver.

We will have to spend all our time keeping these thieving Nubians from stealing it!"

"They look like honest sorts to me," Dave said.

"You don't know them!" Helmut snapped. "Listen, I worked in Nubia two seasons ago near Wadi Halfa. Do you know, the natives stole everything they could get their hands on? They take the treasures to Cairo and sell them on the black market to dealers in antiquities."

Tom thought of the greasy little man near the pyramids who had tried to peddle souvenirs. "Dug up in tombs at Thebes," he had said. But Tom found it hard to believe that these shy, gentle river people were thieves.

"Maybe it was different up there," Tom suggested. "I'm sure Sheikh Ibrahim wouldn't let any of his people steal anything you found."

Helmut laughed. "Sheikh Ibrahim? I think he is an honest man, as these Nubians go. But he cannot be everywhere at once. Let them sniff out gold in that tunnel, and they'll be in there by the dozens."

"You put a gate across the tunnel today," Tom pointed out.

"Will that stop them? "They'll tear it down! I know these people. They'll steal everything and anything!"

"You're being too harsh on them, Helmut," said Roy Fulton. "I don't think they'll go near the tunnel."

"Neither do I" said Janet. "They're probably afraid to set foot in it."

"Wait and see," Helmut warned. "Just wait and see."

Tom was irritated by the fair-haired photographer's insistence that Sheikh Ibrahim's people were criminals. What he had observed so far about the Nubians, he had liked. Maybe in Upper Egypt the villagers rifled tombs, but Tom doubted that the local people would do so. And Janet and Roy seemed to be on his side.

Exciting as the possibilities of the tunnel were, Dr. Falke did not shut down operations on the trading-post site. Ursula and Roy continued to work over there, under Dr. Decker's guidance. Everyone else moved over to the tunnel the following morning.

Tom was impatient to find out what was behind the wall that bore Akhnaten's name and sun-disk symbol. No doubt the others were impatient, too—but Tom quickly learned that there was no plan to take the wall down that day. First, it had to be photographed and sketched. Helmut set up flood-lamps in the tunnel and took several shots of the wall with its crude inscription. Then Janet made sketches, and Kees copied out the hieroglyphics. Finally, each block in the wall received a number, so that, if desired, it could be put up again exactly as it stood originally.

It took nearly the whole day to perform these jobs. Since the work was being done underground, there was no need to quit at midday. Even so, the day's progress seemed maddeningly slight to Tom.

While Helmut, Janet, and Kees were busy with the stone barrier, the others explored the various branches which led out from the first passageway. They went by twos, carrying flashlights: Tom and Holger, Dave and Ted, Dr. Falke and Dr. Marshall. Some of the arteries were short, extending no more than a dozen yards from the main tunnel. Others were long and twisting.

The one Tom and Holger explored turned out to be the longest of all. Holger led the way, paying out a tape measure as he went. Tom studied the walls of the passage, looking for an inscription, a bit of pottery, any sign of former human presence. There was nothing—just the blank sandy walls of the tunnel. It looped round and about several times. Tom began to wonder what would happen if a section of the tunnel fell down behind them and cut them off. Would they ever find their way out again? Would anyone hear them? Or would they be sealed up alive?

"See? The passage ends," Holger said. "The ceiling meets the floor just ahead."

Tom stared into the dimness. Holger was right: the tunnel dwindled away. There was no stone wall here. It simply ended.

Holger examined the far end of the tunnel carefully without finding anything at all. It was apparent that no one had ever made any use of this passageway.

"Why was it built?" Tom asked.

"To confuse thieves," said Holger. "The designers of this tomb wanted to keep the robbers out of the main chambers. So they built many blind alleys and false chambers. Without a light a man would swiftly become lost here." He noted the distance they had come from the main passage in his book, and swiftly sketched an outline of the chamber. Then they turned and made their way back to the others.

By the end of the day, all of the passageways from the main tunnel outside the stone barrier had been explored, and Holger had mapped them. They all turned out to be deliberate snares. Some of them were dead ends; others met and interlocked, so that anyone wandering down one path would eventually emerge on another.

"This whole village must be honeycombed with underground passages," Dave said, looking at Holger's map. "And we're only at the beginning!"

The next day, Holger and Ted began taking down the inner barrier.

They were much more careful with it than they had been with the first stone wall. This one bore inscriptions, and therefore it had archaeological value. Hour after hour, they worked at prying the stones loose and arranging them along the side of the cave, while Janet whitewashed numbers on them so the wall could be restored. Getting the first stone out was the trickiest chore; after that, it was just a matter of sweat and struggle.

When there was a hole in the wall big enough to get both a flashlight and a man's head through, Holger sent for Dr. Falke. The burly expedition leader strode into the tunnel, returning a few minutes later to the group waiting at the entrance.

"Did you see anything?" Kees asked.

"Yes," Dr. Falke said. "I saw more tunnel! It goes on and on. Perhaps it goes all the way to the Red Sea!"

"I understand why the inscriptions were carved so poorly," Kees said with a lopsided grin. "By the time the gravebuilders had finished digging all these tunnels, they were old men. Their hands were shaky when they carved the inscriptions!"

Ali Hosein and Sheikh Ibrahim appeared. They nodded to the archaeologists.

"Well, is there any news?" the Sheikh asked.

"The tunnel continues beyond the wall," said Dr. Falke. "When the wall is down, we shall see what is there."

"Such a long tunnel" said the Sheikh. "Already it is beyond the border of the village."

Ali Hosein said, "They wanted to hide the treasure so no one could find it. When do I go see, Father? I want to see the treasure!"

"We have found no treasure yet," Dr. Falke said, smiling.

Sheikh Ibrahim said, "He will not believe you unless you let him see. May he enter the tunnel?"

"Of course," Dr. Falke said. "Thomas, will you take Ali Hosein in?"

Tom beckoned to the Nubian boy, and went down the steps. The first few dozen yards were easy enough; he simply had to follow the line of electric lights. But then he came to the point where the lights ended, and he had to depend on flashlight illumination. For once, Ali Hosein seemed to have run out of words. As they ventured deeper and deeper into the tunnel, the Sheikh's son became so silent that Tom had to turn around to see if he was still following.

Getting confused only once on the way, Tom traced his way through the tunnel to the wall. The single detour had been a short one: Tom and Ali Hosein wandered into one of the dead-end passages, but it was only twenty feet long, and when they had come around its final bend and had seen the blank sandy barricade, they retraced their steps. The sound of stone being worked gave them their direction, and they were soon back on the right track.

Ted and Holger had removed almost half the barrier. They

113

stopped, resting on their haunches, as Tom and Ali Hosein came up to them.

"Dr. Falke said we could look over the wall," Tom said.

"Go ahead. Look, then," Ted replied.

The tunnel was about six feet high at this point, with the wall still rising a little over a yard from the floor. Tom and Ali Hosein leaned forward, and Tom flashed his light ahead.

It looked like more of the same: five or six branching tunnels, which led in all directions. The flashlight did not reveal any inscriptions.

"I climb over, yes?" Ali Hosein asked. "I see what is in there."

"You'd better not," Tom said. "Your father will be angry with you."

Ali Hosein grinned. "We don't tell him, then!"

He began to slither agilely up the wall. He had one leg thrown over the blocks of stone, and was about to pull the other one over, when Holger reached out with his big paw of a hand and caught Ali Hosein's ankle. The boy tugged but could not get free.

"Come down," Holger ordered. "No one goes in there until Dr. Falke gives his permission."

"You hurt my leg!" Ali Hosein cried.

"I'll let go when you come down from there."

The Nubian boy glared for a moment. But he was caught, and there was nothing he could do but clamber back down. As he slipped from the wall, Holger let go of him.

Ali Hosein looked angry. "I would not damage anything. I only wanted to see."

"I'm sorry," Holger said. "We have rules."

"My father is the Sheikh! This is his village! He——"

"Stop it, Ali," Tom said suddenly. "Even if he *is* the head-man here, Dr. Falke's running the excavation. You know that. It was only a special favor that he let you come in here in the first place."

The anger vanished from Ali Hosein's face as though a button had been pushed. He smiled sheepishly.

"You are right," he agreed. "I do a stupid thing."

He marched over to Holger, who towered more than a foot above him, and looked up at the massive Dane.

"I am sorry," Ali Hosein said. "You are right. I am wrong. I am very stupid sometimes."

Holger shrugged. "When the time comes, you will see what is there. Until then, no. I think you two should go outside again now."

Tom and Ali Hosein started back. When they neared the tunnel entrance, Ali Hosein said, "You will say nothing about what happened?"

"Why should I? It wasn't important."

Tom was inwardly disturbed, though. If Holger hadn't pounced, Ali Hosein would have succeeded in scrambling over the low wall and into the unexplored part of the excavation. That might have caused trouble—and Ali Hosein knew it. His curiosity had overwhelmed him.

Tom couldn't help remembering Helmut's sour words: "I know these people! They'll steal everything and anything!" Tom did not think that Ali Hosein had climbed the wall to steal. But if the Sheikh's son could try to break the rules of the excavation, what would the other boys of the town do?

115

Might they not slip into the tunnel late at night, hop over the wall just as agilely, and——

Tom pushed the thought aside. Helmut was all wrong. No one in the village would do any harm or steal anything from the tunnel.

Assuming there was something to steal, of course. So far, nothing had been discovered but stone walls and dead-end alleys. Tom remembered the stories of the men who had explored the passageways of the pyramids. They had wandered through a maze of intricate tunnels, only to find—nothing at all.

By the end of the day, the inner stone barrier was down. But Dr. Falke ruled that no further exploration would take place until the next day.

"It is enough for now," he said. "If we find something, we will get involved with it and not be able to stop. Tomorrow we will all be fresher."

So the lights were turned off, and the swinging metal gate that had been installed in front of the tunnel entrance was closed. That night, the camp of the archaeologists was subdued. All the arguing and guessing had been done the night before. No one had any idea what the next day might reveal, and there was not much point in making up theories about it.

Dawn came. The sun began to climb across the cloudless blue sky. Flashlights in hand, Dr. Falke and Dr. Marshall led the way into the tunnel once more.

The tunnel grew wider beyond the second stone barrier, so that it was possible to walk two, and even three, abreast. The maze of false passages became more elaborate now. Again and again, the archaeologists found themselves following paths that led nowhere.

Then they came to a new barrier—not a stone wall this time, but simply a heap of rubble, loose chips of sandstone piled so high they blocked the tunnel. It took nearly two hours to clear the rubble away.

"What's behind it?" Tom asked. He was standing well back in the tunnel, keeping out of the way of the busy archaeologists.

"The passageway continues!" Kees called out.

Onward, then. But not very far.

"A doorway!" somebody cried.

"Blocked by bricks!" Holger said.

"Take the picture, Helmut!" boomed Dr. Falke. "Take the picture!"

Tom looked—three slabs of stone set in the wall formed a frame for the doorway. In place of a door rows of bricks were laid from floor to ceiling. Tom did not see how the archaeologists could resist the urge to rip the bricks away and look behind them. But, as always, they remained calm and patient.

They photographed the brick wall. They sketched it. They measured it.

Then Holger peered close. "The bricks are loose," he said. "There is no mortar."

"Pull them out," Dr. Falke said.

Holger worked a brick free, turned and handed it to Kees. He pulled another one free. And another.

"Give me a light," he said.

He shined his flashlight into the opening he had made.

117

"What do you see?" Janet whispered hoarsely.

Holger shrugged. "Darkness. Another wall!"

The tempo of activity picked up. Holger removed row after row of bricks. It was clear now that a second wall lay just within the first. This wall was of brick too, but it had been brushed over with a coating of plaster. And the plaster bore hieroglyphic inscriptions!

Kees came forward and ran his light over the characters. Turning, he said, "It is a hymn to Aten! I think it is the same text as at the tomb of Ay!"

Tom studied the strange characters inscribed in the ancient plaster. Beside him, Ted began to recite the translation of the hymn:

Thy dawning is beautiful in the horizon of heaven,
O living Aten, Beginning of life!
When thou risest in the eastern horizon of heaven,
Thou fillest every land with thy beauty;
For thou art beautiful, great, glittering, high over the earth.

What were they going to do now? Tom wondered. How could they get past the new barrier without destroying the inscription it bore?

He had his answer in a moment. Dr. Falke said, "Janet, can that layer of plaster be separated from the wall behind it?"

"In sections, I think. But we may lose some of it."

"Better than losing all of it. We'll try it."

First, though, the inscription had to be photographed, and copied by hand as well. Janet would then try the delicate and tricky job of peeling the coating of plaster off. It would take many hours.

Most of the archaeologists left the tunnel. It was mid-morning, and it might be late afternoon before anyone knew what lay behind the bricks. Tom was tense and drenched with perspiration. He went down to the river for a swim, then came back to the camp for lunch.

The afternoon dragged on. Word came from the tunnel that Janet was having success in removing the plaster, that much of the original inscription would be preserved. And, once she had finished her work, the wall could be taken down.

It was about five in the afternoon when the excitement began. Tom, unable to watch the painstaking, infinitely taxing process of peeling the plaster coating from the bricks, had settled down at the entrance to the tunnel. Dave had gone inside to watch.

Suddenly, Dave errupted from the tunnel, his eyes wild with astonishment.

"Tom! Roy! Everybody! Come quick!"

"What's happened?" Tom shouted.

"You'll see. Just come!"

He darted back into the tunnel. Tom and the others followed him, racing down the winding, twisted course.

The brick wall had been opened. There was a hole two feet high at the top of the wall. Dr. Falke and the other archaeologists looked dazed, stunned, shaken. Their cool unemotional poise had disappeared.

Dave seized a flashlight and pushed it into Tom's hand. "Look!" he said. "Look in there!"

Tom stood on tiptoe and peered over the topmost row of bricks. He flashed the light ahead. He saw a room, and what looked like some wooden furniture. Then he moved the light a bit to the left.

There was the glitter of gold.

A coffin lay along the wall on one side of the room. It was fashioned in the shape of a man. The figure bore a mask of shining gold. And the face—its features in unmistakable outline—the long jaw, the thick lips, the dreaming eyes——

Only one man in Egypt's history had had a face like that. Akhnaten!

CHAPTER TEN

UNWANTED VISITORS

All work stopped. Dr. Falke called his group together for an urgent conference at the mouth of the tunnel. Tom saw beads of sweat on the expedition leader's forehead. Dr. Falke was trying hard to keep calm, but it clearly was not easy.

Dr. Falke said, "We have discovered something most unexpected, something of major importance. I must ask all of you to maintain secrecy until we have determined where we stand. There must be no premature announcements. First, we must examine the tomb carefully. Then we must communicate with the organizations which have sponsored our expedition. Only when we have done that can we release word of what we have found to the newspapers, magazines, and television stations."

Dr. Falke swung round and looked at Dave. "You, David, are in a very difficult position. I have no legal right to prevent you from cabling this news back to your magazine. I can only request you not to make it public until we are ready to make the announcement."

Tom glanced at his uncle. Dave's face was dark with tension. It was a big story for him, probably the biggest he had ever covered—the finding of the tomb of one of Egypt's most famous pharaohs, a discovery that would answer some of the most troublesome questions in archaeology. It was natural for Dave to want to file his story as early as possible to let the world know of the spectacular find. But if Dr. Falke asked him to wait——

Dave said, "We're here as your invited guests, Dr. Falke. I'll do whatever you wish. I won't release the story until you give me permission."

The archaeologist smiled. "I am grateful for this, David. I will see to it that you are given the exclusive right to tell our story. You will be the official reporter of the expedition. That is the only way I can repay you for your silence now. Is that satisfactory?"

"It's very generous, Dr. Falke."

"So be it, then. As soon as we can lift the communications curtain, David, the story is yours." Dr. Falke looked at the rest of the group. "I hardly need to tell all of you that the secrecy ban applies to you as well. You are to say nothing of this in your letters to friends or family. You are certainly not to get in touch with any publication. Our first duty is to see exactly what we have here; there must be no news given out prematurely. Understood?"

Helmut asked, "Can we tell people that there has been a major find here, if we don't say what *kind* of a find?"

"It is best not to say anything at all," Dr. Falke replied. "No hints, nothing to arouse curiosity. Let the world believe we are excavating old forts and trading posts. I do not want to announce anything until we are aware of what we have actually uncovered." He glanced at his watch. "It is too late to return to work today. Tomorrow morning, we will enter the burial chamber."

"Dr. Falke?" Dave asked for his attention quietly.

"Yes, David?"

"Will you mind if Tom and I watch the work tomorrow?"

"Not at all," Dr. Falke said. "So long as you do not get in the way, you are welcome."

Tom had never spent a longer night. It seemed to him that eternities had elapsed between the time of his first dazzling glimpse of the golden pharaoh and the arrival of morning.

He had slept very little that night. He did not think anyone in the camp had had much sleep. They had been up late, all of them, discussing the incredible discovery. Nobody tried now to deny that they had found Akhnaten's tomb. Not even Kees, so skeptical before, had any doubts. The face on the coffin lid was unmistakable.

In the morning, they entered the tomb again. Since it was something of a special occasion, Dr. Falke relented and called off work on the trading-post site for the time being. Every member of the expedition, accompanied by Tom and Dave, followed the dim electric lights down the long twisting tunnel, past the various obstacles that the tomb builders had set up—down to the burial chamber itself.

Sheikh Ibrahim and Ali Hosein were not with the group that morning. No one had told them that an important find had been made. Dr. Falke preferred to keep the news within the expedition at least for now.

It took Holger and Ted a little more than an hour to take down the brick wall that was the last barrier between the archaeologists and the pharaoh's resting place.

Flashlights flickered as the party filed into the room. The chamber was roughly square—about fifteen feet on each side

—and was cut right out of hard-packed sand. It did not contain many objects. On one side lay some chairs and beds, and an object which looked like a folded-up chariot. Toward the back was a little cluster of statuettes and vases carved from alabaster, a translucent white stone. On the left-hand side of the room stood the coffin.

"They didn't have much time to collect treasures to bury with him," Ted said. "It must have all taken place in a few days—the death of Akhnaten, the preparation of the mummy, the trip to Nubia, the burial."

"Yes," Dr. Marshall said. "None of the pomp and circumstance that usually went with a pharaoh's funeral. They hid him away quickly—before his enemies could get at his body and destroy it."

"It must have taken time to dig this tomb though," Janet said. "All the tunnels, the maze of false passageways——"

"The tomb was made ready in advance, of course," said Dr. Falke. "His followers must have realized it would not have been safe to bury Akhnaten in his own city. So, while he sickened, the digging went on, here in Nubia. There was time to get the tomb ready, but no time to have a proper funeral."

"The coffin must have been designed and built in advance, too," Roy Fulton said. "That looks too elaborate to be a rush job, I'd say."

Tom joined the group standing near the coffin. It was an impressive piece of work. It was about nine feet long and four feet high, carved in the shape of a sleeping man with his arms folded across his breast. The entire coffin was painted the color of gold—but the face itself was a mask of pure beaten gold that had been set in place over the wood. Tom had never seen anything quite so awe-inspiring as the mask of Akhnaten, gleaming in the faint light of the flashlights. The eyes, mere slits, seemed to be gazing into eternity. The forehead was domed, the chin jutting. It was hardly a handsome face. But it seemed almost as though Akhnaten himself lay there, deep in some dream of Aten's mercy. At any moment, the pharaoh might stir, stretch, and sit up, Tom thought.

The room was not big enough for everyone to work at once. Some of the archaeologists left as soon as they had had a good look at the contents. Ursula stepped outside, for there was no pottery for her to examine, and Holger went out, since he could study the design and structure of the burial chamber later when the other work had been done.

Tom and Dave drew away into a corner of the underground chamber and watched the work.

The archaeologists looked like a team of detectives examining the scene of a murder. They were careful not to touch or disturb anything. Helmut set up his camera equipment and proceeded to photograph every nook and cranny of the room from every angle, making a record of its exact appearance at the moment of discovery. Kees crept along the walls looking for inscriptions that might tell the story of the pharaoh's death. Janet sketched the design on the lid of the coffin. Roy and Ted began to examine the wooden furniture to see how much of it could be removed from the tomb without harm.

It was the coffin that fascinated Tom. For thirty-three centuries it had stood untroubled against that cool wall. Was Akhnaten really within? Or was this only a tomb that had been made ready but never actually used?

Dave questioned Dr. Falke. "When will you open the coffin?"

"Oh, a few days from now, perhaps. First, we must clear the furniture away so we have space to work. It will not be an easy job, lifting that coffin lid. Probably there will be other coffins within—one inside the other, like a Chinese puzzle box."

"Do you think Akhnaten's really buried in it?" Tom asked.

Dr. Falke knotted his fingers in his thick beard and tugged at it reflectively. "Ye-e-s," he said slowly. "Yes, I think there is a very good chance of it. The builders of this tomb would not have put so many walls across the passageway if they were not trying to protect something precious."

"The golden mask is precious," Tom said.

"Precious to us. Not to them. Gold was common as dust in Egypt, according to one of the old inscriptions. The mask, the coffin—these would mean nothing to them without the mummy of the king within. But we shall see. A few days more, and we shall see."

"If Akhnaten really is in there," Dave said, "it'll be a discovery of the first magnitude, won't it?"

The archaeologist nodded cautiously. "It would be very important, David. For the first time we would be able to discover the cause of Akhnaten's deformity. An autopsy on the body might reveal the disease that gave him his strange appearance. And, then, we would also be able to settle the question of his age."

"His age?" Tom said, puzzled. "Don't we know how old he was?"

"There are two theories," answered Dr. Falke. "Each is backed by a certain amount of sound evidence. According to

126

one theory, he came to the throne when he was still a child, ruled seventeen years, and died when he was less than thirty. I do not believe this. It would mean that he started his religious revolution when he was a mere boy. The other theory is that he was in his twenties when he became pharaoh, and nearly fifty when he died. The autopsy should give us the answer at last. *If* his body is there, of course. We must not let our hopes run wild."

These archaeologists were a conservative group, Tom thought. Whenever they allowed themselves the luxury of a guess, they immediately hedged it with a lot of *ifs* and *buts* and *maybes*. That was the way it had to be, he knew. These men were scientists. They were not supposed to dream up fanciful theories and then hunt for facts to support them. Their goal was to unearth the facts, then use them as the basis for a theory. The facts came first.

Tom walked toward the coffin again. An early archaeologist, no doubt, would have opened the coffin two hours ago. Dr. Falke and his team knew how to be patient. Before the coffin could be opened, it had to be examined, photographed, sketched, its inscriptions copied, its position in the tomb noted. The worst sin an archaeologist could commit was to rush—because there could never be a second chance, once unique evidence was destroyed through carelessness and impatience.

Tom studied the golden mask. What a masterpiece! He could picture artisans working over it in a mud-walled studio. Had the king himself posed for it? No, probably they had used a portrait of him as their model. The pharaoh would be too busy to pose. They had shaped the gold, hammered it smooth, cunningly given the soft metal the likeness of the king. Skilled fingers had curved those full lips, had rounded the thrusting jaw, had designed the long, slender neck.

Then had come the grim news from the palace. The pharaoh, Akhnaten, was dead! Weeping priests of Aten had hurried the body into the temple for the ancient rite of mummification. The dead king was quickly prepared for the hereafter, for word had come that his enemies were marching from Thebes to seize his capital city. Into the coffin went the mummy of the king. Down went the lid. Did some loyal priest disguise himself as a barge slave to accompany the coffin upriver on its long final journey?

Up the Nile past Thebes to the First Cataract, then, perhaps, overland across the blazing desert—a fearful trek southward along the treacherous river where it could not be navigated. On into Nubia—Akhnaten's last stronghold. Then the burial, the walling up of the tomb. And, at last, back into Egypt to attend the coronation of the new young pharaoh, Tutankhamen.

Had it happened that way? Tom wondered. A cloak-and-dagger operation in dead of night, a king's body smuggled out of the royal capital? Brave men risking their own lives so that the pharaoh might live forever in the hereafter? Tom knew about the Egyptian belief in a life after death. A dead man went to join the gods, becoming part of the company of Re and Osiris.

Akhnaten had not believed in Re and Osiris, had he? But he must have believed there was a life after death. Union with Aten, maybe. An afterlife only if the body survived, though—that was why all Egyptians, even Akhnaten and his followers, had built tombs for themselves to house their mummified bodies. Only if the physical body survived could the soul live again.

The enemies of the king had sought to destroy Akhnaten's body. The friends of the king had saved it. Perhaps. Perhaps. Who knew the secret of this coffin?

Tom leaned forward for a close look at the gleaming golden mask of Akhnaten. It was incredibly beautiful. What would such a work of art be worth? he wondered. No one could set a price. The mask was beyond all price. It was a unique treasure, supremely lovely. Even if the expedition found nothing else, this mask alone would be worth all the toil.

Tom studied the strange features, and a shiver of awe ran down his back. This was the face of Akhnaten. This was the rebel pharaoh himself, staring across time. It seemed to Tom that the mask wore a smile.

There was new excitement when Tom left the tunnel a short while later. The villagers were talking loudly and gesturing upriver in the general direction of Delgo. Ali Hosein came running up to Tom, grinning and leaping, and said, "Your friends are coming!"

"Who? What friends?"

"They landed at Delgo. They come now to visit our village. Many of them. They come from Cairo, your friends. On the big boat."

Tom gave the Nubian boy a blank look. "I don't follow you," he said. "Who are you talking about?"

"Europeans! White men! They must be friends of yours, yes? We are giving them a place to stay. They will be here soon."

Ali Hosein went skipping away. Tom still did not understand at all. Who was coming?

Dave appeared. "What's the excitement about?" he asked.

Shrugging, Tom said, "I've just been trying to find out myself, but I didn't have much luck. Ali Hosein says friends of ours are coming from Cairo. They've just landed on the pier at Delgo. From the big steamer. He says they're Europeans and they're going to stay here awhile."

Dave shook his head. "Who on earth can he mean? We'd better check with Sheikh Ibrahim."

"I haven't seen him."

"He can't be hard to find. Come on."

Tom and his uncle began to walk down into the center of the village. Village boys and girls crept back out of the way, pausing to turn and stare as they went by.

"There he is!" Tom exclaimed.

Dave saluted the village headman. "Sheikh Ibrahim!"

"Peace be with you," the Sheikh said. "Is there trouble in the tunnel?"

"No," Dave said. "But your son told Tom that visitors are coming, friends of ours. We aren't expecting anyone. I wondered if you could tell us who they were."

The Sheikh smiled. "Friends? Ali Hosein must have been inventing stories again. Perhaps they are friends of yours, perhaps not—this I do know. They are simply a group of traveling Europeans. They have come to Nubia to see our monuments, and they have asked to be allowed to stay with us a few days. We have offered them hospitality. I believe they are here now."

He pointed toward the southern end of the village. And, indeed, strangers had appeared. A group of seven or eight

Westerners stood near a mountainous heap of baggage. Nearly all of them were armed with cameras which they were beginning to focus on the village and its inhabitants—to the great distress of the Nubians.

Tom and Dave exchanged stunned glances.

"A band of tourists?" Tom muttered. "*Here?*"

"Just what we need," Dave said. "Dr. Falke is sitting on the discovery of the decade, and these eager-beavers drop in to snoop around. We'll have to hustle them out fast."

"It may not be so easy," Tom said. "Look who's with them!"

A lean figure had detached himself from the group and was coming toward them. Unlike the others, he was dressed simply, in white shirt and khaki slacks. He carried no camera, for he was not a tourist, but the leader of the party. Tom felt a twinge of shock as he recognized the bushy eyebrows, the sharp cheekbones, the thin lips, the cold, glittering eyes.

Paul Kurtz smiled without warmth. "I said we would see one another again," he remarked. "It is really a very small world after all, is it not?"

CHAPTER ELEVEN

THE TROUBLEMAKERS

The archaeologists looked anything but cheerful when they learned of the new arrivals. Dr. Falke's eyes flashed with annoyance and his lips tightened into a thin hard line. Tom got the idea that he would have preferred almost any other kind of trouble at this point—a hurricane, a sandstorm, a plague of locusts—anything except a party of tourists.

But the members of the expedition were forced to be polite and friendly. They did not own the village and they had no right to keep other visitors away. Sheikh Ibrahim was in charge, and Sheikh Ibrahim had made the tourists welcome here—for Nubians were hospitable people.

"They are not to find out anything about the tomb," Dr. Falke said urgently in a low voice. "No one is to say a word about it! We will wait for them to leave before we resume work. We will go back to the trading post and work there until they go. I, personally, will throw anyone into the Nile who lets these people suspect we have found anything."

"But the natives know about the tunnel," Kees pointed out. "What if they say something?"

Dr. Falke sighed and tugged nervously at his beard. "We cannot help that. We have no way of silencing them. But only two of the natives speak a European language—Sheikh Ibrahim and Ali Hosein. I will talk to them. I will ask them to say nothing about the tunnel. Perhaps that will be effective."

The tourists who accompanied Paul Kurtz did not seem to be the same ones he had been leading around Cairo a few weeks before. Not that they were very different, Tom thought. Like the others, these people looked as though they led easy lives. Why they had come to the land of the pharaohs was a mystery. None of them seemed to know much about ancient Egypt, though they had great curiosity about everything they saw. They were constantly peering at people and things, photographing them, reaching out to touch them.

The man who had brought them to Nubia was of another breed. He was slick, sharp, and aggressive. Having shown one group of tourists the pyramids and the temples of Thebes, Paul Kurtz had now collected a new assembly and spirited them off for a look at less familiar sights. The tourists had taken lodging in a group of empty huts at the opposite end of the village from the archaeologists. But it was not long before they began roaming about.

Paul Kurtz had already tried to find out what was going on. Casually, while talking to Tom and Dave, he said, "You've been watching the archaeologists, have you?"

Dave nodded. "Preparing a series of magazine articles. As I told you in Cairo."

Kurtz rocked back and forth on the balls of his feet. "Is there anything interesting to report?"

"An old trading post," Dave said. "I'm sure Dr. Falke will let you take your people over to look at it."

"And you'll want to show them the temple at Delgo, too," Tom said. "With the carvings of Akhnaten on the columns. And I understand there's another temple just down the river from here, at——"

"Yes," Kurtz said coolly. "The temple of Amenhotep III at Sulb. They will see it in due time. But I am wondering if there is something right here in the village that I might show them? Something more interesting than a trading post?"

"I'm afraid not," Dave answered. "It's too bad."

"Indeed, yes. I would have liked to show them a major discovery while it is in the process of being unearthed."

"The trading post is quite interesting," Tom put in. "They can watch the different levels being exposed, and they can see how the archaeologists classify the pottery, and identify the different people who lived in the building——"

Paul Kurtz flashed his quick haughty smile. "I really doubt that it will interest them. They are not trained archaeologists, you understand. They are businessmen—who do not know much about such subtleties; and the wives of businessmen— who know even less." He closed his eyes until they were no more than slits in his lean face. Then he said softly. "On our journey from Delgo, the villagers told me about a strange passageway that had been discovered here. They said the archaeologists had gone down into the depths of the earth and found wonderful things. Is there truth to this, or were they telling stories only to amuse themselves?"

Tom looked at his uncle. "You know anything about any passageways, Dave?"

"Haven't heard a thing. All I know about is the trading post out by the sand dunes."

"Very mysterious," Paul Kurtz said.

"Very," Tom and Dave agreed.

The following morning, Paul Kurtz's party of tourists came out to look at the trading-post site. The entire archaeological expedition was back at work there. No one was stationed at Akhnaten's tomb. The gate in front of the tunnel entrance had been closed, and Dr. Falke had ordered everyone to keep away. He did not want anyone in the visiting group to get suspicious—especially since Paul Kurtz had already heard rumors of a passageway somewhere in the area. They would have to sit tight until the unwanted guests took their leave.

It was frustrating. Down in the underground room lay a wonderful prize, and they could not go near it. One more day, and they might have been able to open the coffin and examine what it contained—but now they had to wait.

It reminded Tom of the time when he was seven years old and his uncle Dave had given him a large, magnificently wrapped box for Christmas. The box had looked as if it held an exciting gift. But Tom had had to wait months to find out what was in it because Dave had given it to him at the beginning of October. He had marked it "DO NOT OPEN UNTIL CHRISTMAS." Then he had gone off to Japan on a magazine assignment.

From the beginning of October to December 25 is a long, long time, especially if you are seven years old and inclined to be impatient. Tom had been tempted many times to sneak a peek at the mysterious box before Christmas. But he had waited. It had been worth the waiting, too. The present had been a marvelous one—a set of beautiful antique tin soldiers from Europe.

Now, down in that winding tunnel, lay another treasure box, and they could not pry into its secrets until Paul Kurtz and company were on their way. It was "Do Not Open Until Christmas," once again. How long would they stay? One day? Two days? Weeks? Months?

It did not take the visitors long to make nuisances of themselves at the trading post. They showed up about eight in the morning, which, apparently, was early in the day for them. The archaeologists, however, had been at work since six. Tom and Dave had joined them, and were helping to dig.

One of the tourist women set the tone for the morning by bellowing loudly: "Where's the ruin? All I see is a hole in the ground!"

"It's just a big sand box," said another woman.

Holger, who was working alongside Tom, looked up sourly at the intruders. "If Dr. Falke had not told us to be polite with these people," he said under his breath, "I would cheerfully stick them headfirst into the sand like ostriches. It would make them less noisy."

"Is that a friendly attitude?" Tom asked.

"No. I do not feel friendly. They are interrupting our work, and——"

"Smile, Holger, and stop grumbling. You're being photographed!"

Click!

Snap!

Whirrrrr!

Cameras were going off like a volley of rifles. One man was taking movies; he called out stage directions to Ursula as he ground away. "Hold up some of those pieces of clay, will you?" he said. "Now, smile! Gee, I didn't know there were any blonde lady archaeologists!"

"Headfirst," Holger muttered darkly. "Deep into the sand, I would put them. Like ostriches!"

Having taken all the pictures they wanted for the moment, the visitors began to roam around the site. So far, no one had actually climbed over the low brick wall to get into the ruined building, but a few of them appeared to be considering it. Even Paul Kurtz looked troubled and embarrassed at their behavior.

Then a pudgy man in yellow knee-length shorts stepped up on the bricks and started to climb over.

Dr. Falke appeared, a look of great patience on his bearded face, and stopped him with a commanding boom: "I'm sorry, but it will not be possible for you to enter the site."

"I just want to get a couple of pictures close up," the man said. "And I'd like to get a shot of my friends from inside."

"Sorry. There is danger of your disturbing the strata, and I will have to ask you——"

"Mr. Slocombe," Paul Kurtz interrupted. "Would you please come away from there? We mustn't bother Dr. Falke, you know. It's a great favor that we're here at all."

The intruder hesitated, looking disgruntled, and then obeyed the order.

Dr. Falke turned away. Tom saw him roll his eyes heavenward as though asking for strength to survive the invasion. Paul Kurtz called his group back a little way and began to deliver a lecture on the methods of archaeologists. He seemed to know the subject thoroughly. He explained why the site was cut down to expose all the different levels, touched on the importance of the pottery fragments, and described what each member of the expedition was doing. The tourists did not seem very interested, but they kept out of everyone's way while the guide was talking to them.

When Kurtz finished, they prowled around the excavation site a bit longer and took a few more photographs. Then the crowd left, having found nothing to hold their interest any longer.

"Are they really gone?" Kees asked. "Will they come back again?"

"I try to be cooperative with visitors where I work," Dr. Falke said. "But these people——they know nothing, they understand nothing, they listen to nothing!"

"I don't like that guide of theirs," Janet remarked. "He gives me the creeps, with those eyebrows of his, and those dead-looking eyes."

"A walking mummy?" Tom suggested.

"Whatever he is, he's sneaky-looking. I wish he'd pack up and clear out, and take his tribe with him," Janet said.

Holger clenched and unclenched his big fists. "Into the sand," he said in a low voice. "Headfirst. Like ostriches. That is what I would do!"

The tourists did not leave. They had seen all they wanted to see at the trading post, but they were remaining at the village—at least, for another few days.

That afternoon, Kurtz took them across to view the temple at Delgo. It was good to have them out of the village, at any rate. Tom wondered what pleasure these people could possibly get out of roaming around under the fierce Nubian sun, staring at shattered monuments of no real interest except to students or Egyptologists. To say they had been somewhere that few tourists visited, he decided, was the only reason they could have for coming here. Perhaps they would leave when they had seen the nearby temples.

In the afternoon, while the tourists were away, Ali Hosein called Tom inside. The Nubian boy said, "Your friends—they are not really your friends, are they?"

"No. I don't know them and I don't like them."

"I am glad. I don't like them, either. They are stupid and noisy. And all the time with the camera—why so many pictures? In our villages we do not like the pictures being taken."

"They'll go away soon," Tom said. "And then we can go back to working on the tunnel."

Ali Hosein grinned. "You don't want the new ones to find out about the tunnel?"

"No. Dr. Falke's afraid they'll make trouble if they find out."

"They steal the treasure, eh?" Ali Hosein suggested.

Tom didn't know how much Sheikh Ibrahim and his son had been told about the room at the end of the tunnel, so he said, "Well, they'd get in the way. Dr. Falke doesn't want them to bother him."

"The ugly-faced one asks many questions," Ali Hosein said. "He speaks our language. He asks the boys about your friends. He wants to know: is there a tunnel somewhere? is there treasure in it? All kinds of questions."

Tom stiffened. "What have they been telling him?"

"Some say *yes*, some say *no*. He is all mixed up."

"Good," Tom said. "Keep him mixed up."

The news that Paul Kurtz was nosing around the village for information about the archaeologists was hardly encouraging.

139

Sooner or later, Tom thought, he would find out about the passageway and what it contained, and then the roof would blow off!

At dinner that evening, as the ten archaeologists, Tom, and Dave were sitting at the same table, Tom brought up the news Ali Hosein had given him. "Paul Kurtz has been quizzing the village boys. Ali Hosein says he speaks Nubian."

Holger pounded the table with a massive fist. "We must throw them out of here fast!"

"We can't do that," objected Dr. Marshall. "But if he keeps sniffing around, he's bound to figure out that we're hiding something from him."

"We'll never get rid of him if that happens," Roy Fulton said. "He'll just stay and stay and stay until he uncovers the truth."

Dr. Falke scowled and knotted his fingers together tensely. "His people will get restless. They will be gone in another day, I think."

"What if he finds out about the tomb?" Ted Clay asked. "Suppose he gets the story and sends it to some newspaper? It'll come out in a garbled version, and everything will get confused and tangled. You know what I think? We ought to release the news right now. Let Dave write up a story and cable it to his publishers. That way the first announcement will come from us, instead of some skulking jackal of a touristmonger."

All eyes were on Dr. Falke. He shook his head negatively. "No," he said. "I see your point, Ted. But we cannot rush. How do you say it? We cannot jump the gun. Until we know what that coffin contains, we must not announce anything. And we cannot look into the coffin until our visitors depart."

"Just a preliminary announcement," Ted said. "News of finding a tomb and a coffin. No need to talk about Akhnaten or even about the gold mask."

"We wait," Dr. Falke said. "We wait until they leave."

Tom said quietly to Dave, "Maybe you ought to speak up. If this fellow Kurtz steals your scoop——"

"Dr. Falke's in charge," Dave said firmly. "We'll just have to hope Kurtz will pack his bags and move along without making trouble. I'm not sending out any stories until I have official permission. That's final."

That was where the matter rested. The following morning, Ali Hosein reported that the visitors were going to stay in the village at least one more day. They were off to see the temple at Sulb today, and would return to the village late in the afternoon. Tomorrow, maybe, they would move on.

A short while afterward, Paul Kurtz came up to the trading-post site—without his band of tourists. The archaeologists were once again at work there, gloomily going through their dreary tasks while the much more exciting project of exploring the tomb remained suspended.

Kurtz trudged to the wall of the trading post and asked, "May I speak with you, Dr. Falke?"

The expedition leader glanced up. "Go ahead."

"In private, perhaps?"

"I have no secrets from my friends here," Dr. Falke said irritably. "What do you want?"

Kurtz's face went taut for a moment, but he quickly slipped his smile back into position. "Very well, then. I will tell you.

In the village, I have heard stories that you have made an important discovery here. Not this trading post, but something much more important. There is talk of a tunnel, a passageway. They have shown me the gate you put up across an opening in the ground, and they say this is the entrance. Are these just village lies? What is that gate, Dr. Falke?"

There was a long moment of silence. Tom saw Dr. Falke's eyes grow hard. He tugged furiously at his beard. Finally, he replied. "There is a tunnel, yes. We opened it and explored it. It contains empty passageways and many false paths." He went no further. What he had said, Tom thought, was perfectly true. Dr. Falke did not want to lie, even to Paul Kurtz.

Kurtz said, "Is that *all* though? Nothing in it?"

"Herr Kurtz, may we continue our work in peace?" Dr. Falke said. "I think we have given you much of our time already. Now I must ask you———"

"I'm only trying to offer my services," Kurtz said. "I'm a newspaperman as well as a tourist guide. I have connections all over Europe. If you've discovered something important, let me handle the announcement for you. I'll write it up accurately—not like a lot of people would. And———"

Dr. Falke cut him off. "Over there," he said frostily, "is Mr. David Lloyd. He is also a journalist. In the event that we have any news here, Herr Kurtz—in the event, I say—Mr. Lloyd will receive the privilege of telling the world about it. That has already been arranged. We have no need of your services. Good day, Herr Kurtz. Good day."

And, for the first time since Tom had known him, Dr. Falke was deliberately rude. The deep-voiced archaeologist glared at Kurtz, then turned his back on him.

Kurtz stood gaping for a moment. The look on his face was venomous. He closed his mouth, squared his shoulders, drew himself up rigidly. Then, without a word, he swung around and walked away furiously.

CHAPTER TWELVE

THE OPENED GATE

The next day, Paul Kurtz and his tourists were still quartered in the village. They had seen both the temples in the neighborhood, and they had watched the archaeologists at work at the trading post. There was nothing else for them to see or do here—unless they thought that Dr. Falke was hiding something from them. Yet they remained.

Tension was mounting in the camp of the archaeologists. The scientific group was eager to get back into the tunnel and continue work on the tomb. But so long as the intruders stayed, the gate across the tunnel mouth remained closed.

"Why don't they leave?" Ursula demanded impatiently. "What are they staying for?"

"They've found out there's something important in the village tunnel," Holger answered. "They are waiting for us to go back to work there. It is a waiting game."

"I doubt it," Dr. Falke said mildly. "I think it is a much simpler matter. They are waiting for the next steamer to arrive at Delgo. It is not due for several days. Until then, they stay here. It is unfortunate for us, but not really serious."

Tom had to admit that Dr. Falke's theory made sense. The

144

tourists had satisfied their curiosity about this part of Nubia. They kept close to their huts, looking irritated and bored, as if they were anxious to be somewhere else. Maybe they were simply waiting for the steamer to take them away.

Tom tried to relax. It was not easy. Paul Kurtz and his herd had been in the village four days already. Tom felt as if he had been holding his breath all that time. If only they would leave and let the work start again in Akhnaten's tomb!

Tom was too restless to spend much time out at the trading-post site. He tried working off his edginess by walking through the village. The villagers were losing their shyness toward him. Probably the presence of the newcomers had something to do with that, he thought. The new arrivals made the "old" strangers seem almost like long-time residents, and few natives fled when he came strolling through the rows of gaily decorated mud buildings. There were smiles and soft murmurs of welcome.

Tom passed most of the morning with Ali Hosein. The Sheikh's son talked a blue streak, but he was a lively and interesting companion. They walked down to the river.

"See where the water is rising?" Ali Hosein asked.

"Is the dam doing that?"

"Mostly it is the flood," Ali Hosein explained. "The water comes down the mountains now. Two months ago all was dry here. We planted vegetables where the river now runs. Next year we will not be able to do that. The new dam will hold the water all year instead of letting it run to the sea. The river will be much higher. And the year after that, we all must move."

"The village will be covered with water?" Tom asked.

"Half of it will. So we all move. We go south together. Everything will be flooded here—up to *there*." He indicated a point well back from the shore. The tunnel of Akhnaten's tomb was one of the places that would be engulfed, Tom saw. But by then, hopefully, the archaeologists would have finished their underground work. How lucky they had been to stumble across such a miraculous find in the next-to-last possible season! In two more years, it would have been hidden forever.

Tom asked, "Do you feel unhappy about moving?"

Ali Hosein grinned. "The old people do. Why should I? Maybe they move us to America instead of to the south, yes? They move us to New York." He laughed and clapped his hands in pleasure at his own idea. "You have a river near New York? We live there! A Nubian village in New York, yes?"

"It gets cold there," Tom said. "It snows in the winter."

"Snows? I do not understand."

"Like rain," Tom said. "It comes down from the sky. But not water. It comes down like—like——" He groped for the word he wanted. "Like *snow*," he said finally. "Soft white stuff, very cold. It melts when you touch it and turns to water."

Ali Hosein's eyes were very wide, and his shining black forehead was corrugated in puzzlement. "Snow?" he repeated, mystified. "Like rain? Melts?" He laughed softly. "I do not understand. It comes from the sky?"

"In cold weather. When it's warmer, rain comes down. Drops of water."

"All the time?"

"No, only when—when it's raining," Tom said lamely.

146

"Water collects in the clouds, and when there's enough of it, it falls. But in cold weather it comes down as snow. Little white flakes. They pile up everywhere. The whole world turns white for a while."

"It is like a dream. Everything white! Snow—like the desert sand! Someday maybe it happens here and I see, yes?"

"Not very likely," Tom said. "It has to be cold, really cold. Like—like the bottom of the river, only even colder. I don't think it's ever snowed in Africa, except maybe at the tops of the highest mountains."

Ali Hosein bubbled with questions. Snow fascinated him. Could you eat it? Could you keep it in your house to play with? Could you lie down in it?

Tom tried to help him understand. But he realized that Ali Hosein was not comprehending at all. How could you explain snow to someone who was hardly able to imagine rain? What did the idea of "coldness" mean to Ali Hosein? How could he grasp the picture of frozen flakes of water falling from the sky? Tom sensed the huge gulf that separated him from this Nubian boy. They came from different worlds. Yet he felt that the gulf could be bridged somehow. Ali Hosein was intelligent. His mind worked with frightening speed. Tom watched him struggling with the notion of snow, the way a blind man might try to understand the meaning of color. He was making a real effort. Tom helped all he could. Even so, as they walked back from the shore to the village, Tom was not sure that Ali Hosein had actually grasped the strange concept.

"I see you later," Ali Hosein called, and went skipping away toward his home.

147

Tom waved to him and started for the camp of the archaeologists. It was nearing midday. Now that he had been in the Nile region a few weeks, Tom hardly noticed the terrific heat any more. Still, he did not want to be outdoors at noon.

His route took him past the hut which had been built above the entrance to Akhnaten's tomb. Automatically, Tom glanced at the tunnel entrance which was blocked by a locked gate. He thought of the excitement a few days before when the tomb had been entered. Now the archaeologists were deliberately keeping far away from the tunnel, so as to avoid stirring up the curiosity of Paul Kurtz. Maybe, in another few days——

Tom stopped short. He took a second look at the gate across the tunnel mouth.

Was it—*no!* YES!

THE GATE WAS OPEN!

Tom ran to it. The lock had been a flimsy one, and someone had broken it! Whoever had done it had carefully left the lock in its place, but it protected nothing now. The gate was open. Anyone could nudge it aside and enter the tunnel that led to Akhnaten's tomb!

Tom froze in his tracks. A dozen thoughts whirled through his mind at once. He wanted to rush into the tunnel and make certain that everything was safe. But he knew that he had no business going in there alone, that he should get the archaeologists at once. Yet he didn't want to leave the gate open and rush up to their camp, for who knew who might sneak into the tunnel while he was gone?

So he did nothing for a moment. Heart pounding furiously, Tom stood there in the sun's blaze, staring at the broken lock. A sudden breeze came up, and hot screaming sand whistled past his cheeks. He caught sight of a tall man crossing between two huts a few hundred yards away, and yelled.

"Holger! Holger, come here—fast!"

The brawny archaeologist came trotting toward him. "What's the matter, Tom?"

"Look!"

"The lock!" Holger gasped. "Have you been inside?"

"I just found it that way. I haven't touched a thing!"

"Get Dr. Falke and the others. I'll stay here and keep guard."

"Right."

Tom sprinted up the slight slope that led from the tunnel mouth to the camp of the archaeologists. It was a short run, but he was faint and dizzy from the heat by the time he came stumbling into the room where the expedition members were just starting lunch.

"There's trouble!" Tom blurted.

Everyone whirled. Dr. Falke said, "What is the matter, Thomas?"

Tom pointed down the hill. "The tunnel—the lock—someone's forced the lock——!"

Tom had never seen a group of people move so fast. The words were hardly past his lips when the archaeologists sprang to their feet and started bolting past him. He was nearly trampled in the rush. Dave was the last one out, and he caught Tom by the arm and dragged him along.

Holger grimly guarded the useless gate. He had not entered

the passage. Dr. Falke shouldered his way forward and knelt to inspect the lock. There was a terrible silence. At last, he rose and said quietly to Dr. Decker and Dr. Marshall, "Let us go inside and see what has been done. The rest of you wait out here."

The three archaeologists disappeared into the tunnel. None of the group standing outside spoke. The noon sun beat down, baking them mercilessly. No villagers were around, for it was the middle of the day. From the distance came the faint sound of laughter: the tourist group, having lunch in a hut at the other end of the village.

It seemed a century before the three men returned. They came up out of the tunnel wearing the longest faces Tom had ever seen.

"Nothing's been damaged," Dr. Marshall said. "Everything's untouched and all right."

"Except for the golden mask," added Dr. Falke. "The mask is gone!"

It was a somber group of archaeologists that discussed the shocking news. The mask stolen! The funeral mask of Akhnaten!

Helmut pounded his fist into his hand. "I told you this would happen. These natives steal anything! It was the same at the last site I worked. They have sensitive noses. They can smell gold a mile away."

"We put a gate up," Ted said.

"A gate, a gate!" Helmut sneered. "What good is a gate? A flimsy little thing like that? The pharaohs hid their tombs behind tons of stone, and still these people found them and robbed them!"

Dr. Falke said, "We'll speak to Sheikh Ibrahim. If one of the natives has stolen the mask, he will help us recover it, certainly."

"Absurd," Helmut said. "The mask's already on its way north. It's probably halfway to Aswan by now. Next week, it'll be in Cairo, and some rich collector will pay a hundred thousand dollars for it on the black market; then it'll never be seen again! What good will questioning Sheikh Ibrahim do?"

"Perhaps the mask is still here," Dr. Falke said quietly.

"We don't even know that the villagers are guilty," Tom said. "What about Kurtz and his tourists? Maybe one of them wanted a souvenir."

Kees laughed. "Those heavy-bellied fools? How could they fit inside the tunnel?"

"Kurtz could," Tom said. "Why not ask *him* about the mask? Search his luggage? He——"

"No," Dr. Falke said. There was a note of finality in his voice. "We have no right to search anyone's luggage."

"We could question them, at least," Tom persisted.

"Then they would know what's in the tomb," said Dr. Marshall. "If they aren't the thieves, we'll be handing away the information we've been trying to keep from them."

"It is the Nubians who have done this," Helmut said. "I am positive of it!"

Dr. Falke shrugged. "I will talk to Sheikh Ibrahim about it. Meanwhile, we must take steps to guard the tomb against further entry. Dr. Marshall tells me that we do not have any other locks. It will take days to get new ones from Cairo. So we must post round-the-clock guards at the entrance to the tunnel."

"We should have done that from the start," Helmut said. "A gate wasn't good enough."

Dr. Falke allowed a little impatience to show. "It is too late for hindsight now, Helmut. But from now on, we will guard the entrance. There are ten of us, so if we stand guard on three-hour shifts——"

"There are twelve of us, Dr. Falke," Dave said. "Tom and I will help you stand guard."

"This is no concern of yours," said Dr. Falke. "I can't ask you to expose yourselves to possible danger. If someone tries to force his way into the tomb there could be trouble."

"We're willing to take that risk," Tom said. "The more there are to share the job, the easier it'll be for everyone. And it *is* our concern. At least, I think so."

Dave nodded in agreement. "So do I. Let us help, Dr. Falke."

"Very well. Twelve of us—a two-hour shift, then, once every twenty-four hours, for each of us. And I will have Sheikh Ibrahim question his people. Perhaps we will still recover the mask."

"It is really not very important," said Dr. Decker in an odd voice. "We have photographs of the mask. It is a lovely piece of work, yes, but do we need the original mask any more except for a museum piece?"

"You have always felt that way about such things, Heinrich," said Dr. Falke. "But there are others who regard the mask as more important than you do, I'm afraid."

"Such as the Sudanese Department of Antiquities," Kees pointed out. "The mask belongs to them, let's not forget. We'll be held responsible for its disappearance."

"I knew it would happen!" Helmut muttered. "I knew it! The villagers are nothing but common thieves!"

Lots were drawn for the sentry assignments. Holger got the first two-hour stint. Tom drew three to five in the morning as his duty. A couple of the archaeologists thought it was unfair for a guest to have to serve such uncomfortable hours, but Tom refused to trade with anyone. He explained that, since he got up around five each morning anyway, he'd simply wake up a couple of hours before that, and then take a nap during the middle of the day. Besides, he said, he'd be standing guard in the cool of the night, which was a lot better than having to do so under the full blast of the midday sun, as Holger would have to do.

Tom was stunned by the theft. The exquisite, glittering, mysterious mask gone! He could not take the loss as lightly as Dr. Decker. The German archaeologist was mainly interested in what could be learned from a site, not in the antiquities it could yield for museums. All right—that was the modern attitude. Even so, Tom thought, didn't the man's soul tingle at the sight of that mask? Didn't he feel even a pinch of excitement at beholding such a masterpiece?

Helmut was still insisting that one of the villagers had stolen it. He was making quite a bore of himself with his repeated accusations. Was it possible, Tom wondered, that the Nubians were guilty?

He didn't like the idea. He was fond of Ali Hosein, who was the only Nubian he really knew, and he didn't want to think that one of Ali Hosein's people had committed the theft. And yet, hadn't Ali Hosein himself talked endlessly about the "treasure" that he "knew" was in the tunnel? Maybe the other Nubians had talked about treasure, too— until one of them decided to take a look, and slipped into the unguarded tunnel while no one was watching.

Tom remembered how Ali Hosein had tried to clamber over the low wall inside the tunnel. If Holger hadn't grabbed him and pulled him back, he would have gone over. And Ali Hosein knew the rules. He knew he wasn't supposed to climb over walls without Dr. Falke's permission. That hadn't stopped him from trying. Other villagers might have even more careless or defiant attitudes toward the rules of the archaeologists.

Dr. Falke was gone a long time. In the camp, the members of the expedition stared gloomily at one another.

"It is going to be difficult for Dr. Falke if the mask doesn't turn up," Kees said. "He'll have to report the theft to the Department of Antiquities. They'll want to know why he didn't post guards in the first place. They could even suspect him of stealing the mask himself and pretending that the villagers took it. If they get angry enough with him, they may never let any of us come back to Nubia to work. And the Egyptian officials will react the same way."

"It'll be the Nefertiti head all over again," Janet said.

Tom turned to her. "What do you mean?"

"You've seen pictures of the head of Queen Nefertiti that was found in Akhnaten's city, haven't you?"

"Yes, of course," Tom said, thinking of the queen's strikingly beautiful face and swanlike neck. It was a famous work of art. There was a photograph of it in nearly every book on Egypt Tom had looked at.

Janet went on. "It's in the Berlin Museum today. An archaeologist named Borchardt found it in 1912. He was supposed to turn it over to the Egyptian authorities. By law, everything that archaeologists find in Egypt belongs to the Egyptian government. The Department of Antiquities decides which things the archaeologists can take home with them and which must stay in Egypt. Borchardt knew that they'd never let him keep the head of Nefertiti. It was too beautiful. So he didn't report it. He smuggled it out of Egypt and it was displayed in Berlin."

"How did the Egyptians react to that?" Tom asked.

"They were furious. There was practically an international incident over it. They demanded Nefertiti back, but the Germans kept her anyway. For many years afterward, no German archaeologist could get permission to dig in Egypt. If the Sudanese and Egyptian governments get the idea that Dr. Falke is pulling a fast one with the mask of Akhnaten, he may go on the blacklist too. It would be the end of his career as an Egyptologist."

"Maybe the end of our careers too," Kees said. "We've got to find that mask, even if Dr. Decker thinks it doesn't matter much."

"We will never find it," said Helmut darkly. "It is already hundreds of miles from here. We will never see it again."

"Don't be such a pessimist," Tom told him. "Maybe some village boy took it as a souvenir, and will give it back if Sheikh Ibrahim asks him. Maybe——"

A shadow appeared in the doorway. Dr. Falke entered. He looked preoccupied and worried.

"Sheikh Ibrahim was shocked by the news," Dr. Falke said. He stared coldly at Helmut. "The Sheikh does not believe that anyone in his village would have stolen the mask.

But he will question the villagers. He said he would speak to everyone in the village—one by one. If there is a thief among the villagers, Sheikh Ibrahim will find him."

"And if the thief's already on his way to Cairo with the mask?" Helmut asked.

"The Sheikh will know if anyone is missing," Dr. Falke answered. "We will have the answer soon enough."

CHAPTER THIRTEEN

FOOTSTEPS IN THE NIGHT

It was five minutes to three in the morning. Tom came walking slowly down the sandy path that led from his hut to the tunnel entrance. The little alarm clock Dr. Falke had given him had rung only for a few seconds before Tom snapped it off so it would not awaken Dave. It was almost time for him to stand watch.

Ted Clay sat by the mouth of the tunnel, reading a book by the pale glow of moonlight. He closed the book and yawned as Tom approached.

"Three o'clock and all's well," Tom said softly. "Go catch some sleep."

"Sure," Ted said sourly. "Three hours of sleep and then it's time to go to work. A great life!"

Tom managed a grin. He settled down in the sand next to the tunnel mouth, and Ted went trudging back to his hut. The world was wonderfully silent at this early hour. No one was stirring in the village; no birds shrieked overhead. It was so still that Tom could hear the sound of a faint breeze ruffling the palm fronds near the edge of the river. It was cool, too. Peaceful. The village slept.

Stifling a yawn, Tom leaned back against the mud wall of

the building and looked at the star-studded sky. His eyes felt raw; he hadn't slept much during the short night. It had been past eleven when he had finally touched head to pillow, and then he had had to wake before three. Less than four hours of sleep—not enough, not nearly enough. His eyelids felt heavy. His head kept sagging forward.

Careful, now, he warned himself. *No drowsing! No snoozes on sentry duty!*

Two hours to go. At five, Kees would come to relieve him. He'd be free to go back to sleep then, if he wanted to—although dawn would be breaking, and it would be more sensible to stay awake and do his sleeping between ten and two o'clock. Two hours. A hundred and twenty minutes. How many seconds was that? Seven thousand, two hundred, was it? That wasn't so many. Why, already dozens of seconds had gone by. A hundred eighteen minutes to go—a hundred seventeen minutes——

Suddenly Tom began to feel very sleepy.

Stay awake! he ordered himself. *No napping, do you hear? What kind of watchman are you?*

He looked out at the slumbering village. Was the mask of Akhnaten hidden in one of those brown mud huts? Was some light-fingered Nubian smirking in his sleep as he dreamed of the wealth that now was his?

All during the afternoon, Sheikh Ibrahim had questioned his people. Tom had seen the line of villagers filing through the Sheikh's house. To some, Sheikh Ibrahim had spoken only for a moment; others had been questioned for many minutes. An air of tension had descended on the village. Everyone knew now that something valuable had been stolen. The villagers were eyeing each other suspiciously. Tom saw them whispering, pointing.

Sheikh Ibrahim had had no luck. "I have talked to them all," he reported to the archaeologists after dinner. "No one has left the village. Everyone denies doing this thing. There are a few I will speak with again tomorrow. Their eyes did not meet mine when I questioned them. But I do not think we will find the thief in my village."

Even the tourists, snug in their huts at the far end of the village, sensed that something was wrong. They came out to peer around and murmur to one another. Happily, they were leaving the following day. The steamer would call at Delgo shortly after noon. One of the tourists—the man who had tried to climb into the trading-post site—had sauntered up to find out why the natives were being questioned.

"Why the grilling?" he asked. "They take something?"

"It's a village matter," Ted Clay told him. "Nothing of any real importance."

"Looks like a police line-up to me. Somebody stole somebody's goat, huh?"

"Something like that," Ted answered vaguely.

Now, hours later, Tom wondered if they ever would find the thief—or the missing mask. There were no police in the village. The village sheikh maintained law and order. There were no detectives, no sleuthing equipment. What was the use of searching for fingerprints on the lock or within the tomb itself? Nobody kept files of fingerprints in Nubia. Even if they found prints, there would be no way of identifying them. They could only trust to luck, hope that Sheikh Ibrahim would be able to find the guilty man and get the precious mask returned unharmed—assuming it was a villager who had stolen it, of course. Tom still found that idea hard to buy.

He yawned again. Sleep was creeping up on him. Shaking his head, Tom tried to force himself to stay awake. Ten minutes had passed already. Only ten? An hour and fifty minutes to go. It seemed like forever.

Dawn would come. The first pink streaks would stain the sky, and then the sun would burst out of the east. By that time, his shift would be over. All he had to do was stay awake till five. All he—had—to—do—was——

Was——

Was—stay—awake——

He struggled against sleep. He told himself to get up, walk around, do some deep knee bends and pushups. But he stayed where he was. His head lolled. His eyelids were getting heavy, so very heavy——

He slipped into a half doze; he was not really asleep, but not fully awake either. Somewhere in the drowsy depths of his mind Tom knew that he was doing a bad job as a watchman and that he'd better straighten up and come to attention. But he couldn't. He slipped deeper into sleep from moment to moment.

Strange figures began to move to and fro behind his closed lids. Akhnaten was there, oddly majestic despite his strange appearance, seated on a throne of gold. Nefertiti was at his side, a lovely woman of queenly grace. There were courtiers bowing to the pharaoh. Incense curled upward from a golden pot. Priests were chanting a hymn; strangely, Tom was able to understand the words: they were praising Aten, who looked after the fish in the Nile, the chickens unhatched in the egg, the cattle grazing in the green fields. Now Akhnaten was rising from his throne, spreading his hands forward as though to give a blessing, and——

WHAT WAS THAT NOISE?

Tom sat bolt upright. His eyes fluttered open. He had heard a squeaking sound—the gate of the tunnel being pushed back! And footsteps! Soft padding footsteps as someone slipped past him and down the passageway!

Tom sprang to his feet. Staring into the tunnel, he caught sight of a figure in white. White robe, dark skin—a Nubian! Sneaking into the tunnel to steal again!

"Hey!" Tom called. "Hey, you there! Come back, whoever you are! Come out of there!"

The intruder paid no attention. He reached the elbow in the tunnel, rounded it, and disappeared. Tom's cheeks blazed with shame. A fine guard he had been! The thief had come back, looking for more loot, and Tom had been dozing like a graybeard. What would he have said to the archaeologists if he had not awakened and something else had been stolen? He would not have been able to face them.

But luck was with him. He had a chance to redeem himself. The thief was somewhere in the tunnel. There was no time to call for help, or to run back to the camp to fetch the others. Tom knew that the thief had to be caught before he reached the pharaoh's tomb. Otherwise he might do great damage in his hasty search for something precious enough to steal.

Tom ran down the steps of the tunnel. The thief was trapped, he thought jubilantly. The tunnel had only one entrance, and that was also the only exit. He would catch the intruder and drag him to Dr. Falke.

There was no sign of the white-clad figure now. The twists

and turns of the tunnel made it impossible for Tom to see more than ten or fifteen feet ahead at any time. He was not helped much by the flickering yellow light of the electrical system. Those faint bulbs gave next to no light at all.

Tom was past the place where the first stone wall had been.

Now a number of passages faced him, but he followed the one that had the electric lights strung along the ceiling. That was the path that led to the tomb of the pharaoh. The others were dead ends.

But when he had gone another thirty feet, Tom hesitated, frowning. What if the thief had slipped into one of the dead-end passages to hide? That way, while Tom went plunging past down the main route, the thief could slip out and make his escape. On the other hand, if Tom stopped to explore the side alleys, the thief might reach the tomb and harm the coffin.

What to do? He couldn't guard the tomb and explore the side paths at the same time.

But he would have to try to do both, he decided. He backed up a bit and peered into one of the other passages. No one had strung any lights in there, and in his hurry Tom had left his flashlight by the entrance to the tomb. Still, he could see a little way into the opening. There didn't seem to be anyone there. Tom held his breath and listened for the sound of breathing. All was silent.

Tom moved on. He glanced into two other passages. No sign of anyone. Probably the thief had gone straight to the burial chamber. Since he had been here before to steal the mask, he knew that he simply had to follow the line of electric lights and ignore the dark openings in the wall.

Wide awake now, heart racing furiously, Tom crept forward. Every time he came to a bend in the tunnel he paused and tried to see around the corner. The thief knew he had been seen. He might be waiting there to ambush Tom. Tom clenched his fists in readiness. He came to the place where the second stone wall had been. It was not much further to the tomb now. The thief was somewhere ahead, and in another moment Tom would catch up with him.

Then the lights went out.

It happened quickly. The lights faded away to a ghostly glow, then blazed, then faded a second time. And did not glow again. The little generator that powered them had chosen the worst of all possible times to break down!

Tom took a couple of steps in the dark, then stopped, waiting, hoping that his eyes would adjust. They didn't. This wasn't a movie theater, where there was some light to see by. This was a tunnel deep under the desert. Tom was in total blackness.

But so was the thief. They were on even terms there.

And, Tom thought, maybe he had a small advantage over the other. He knew he could find his way around in the dark by reaching up and feeling for the electrical wires. So long as he kept contact with them, he'd know that he was still in the main passage and not off in some blind alley. Would the thief think of that? Tom hoped not.

He wondered what to do now. Turn around and go back, grope his way out of the tunnel, and get help? Maybe that was the best idea. The robber couldn't do much damage in the pitch dark, anyway.

The first thing to do, at any rate, was to find the electrical wires to serve as a guide. Tom reached toward the low ceiling of the tunnel and groped around. They ought to be along

163

the right side of the tunnel wall, held by brackets. Right over here, he said to himself.

He felt nothing.

Strange, he thought. He put his hand against the wall and swept it in an arc from left to right. Somewhere along that arc, the electrical cord should be.

Nothing.

Where was it? Tom's flesh began to crawl as he realized what must have happened. In the second the lights went out, he must have gone forward a few steps—just far enough to take him out of the main path and into one of the side ones. There was no electrical installation here. He had nothing to guide him. He was lost in the labyrinth of passageways. Somewhere—ahead of him or behind him, he had no way of knowing—was a desperate thief. But where?

Tom swung round. There was no sense in going straight ahead and getting even more lost than he already was. If he could find the main path again——

Step by step, he edged forward, his hands groping along the ceiling as he went. The blackness was so intense that it hurt his eyes. It was like having a hood over his head, he thought. Step by step by step. Where was the light cord? Surely he was back in the main passage by now, wasn't he? Or had he gone two steps too far, and blundered across into another false turn? He remembered how he and Holger had explored these passageways, some of them with dead ends, others that curved back upon themselves and fed into still other blind alleys. If the thief got past him while he stumbled around in here, if the thief slipped away and escaped, Tom would have a hard time telling the archaeologists what had happened.

He took another step.

Another.

Another.

Still no wires bracketed to the walls. That meant he was still in one of the false alleys. And, probably, getting further and further from the main path with every step. He had no idea of which way the main tunnel was now. Right or left, ahead or behind—all directions seemed to blur into one.

Tom stopped. He tried to take his bearings—without the slightest success. Then he caught his breath sharply. Noise! The soft sound of breathing, ahead. Someone coming toward him. Footsteps scuffling along. Leaning forward into the darkness, Tom tried to see through the black wall before his eyes, but it was like trying to see through stone. He waited, motionless, breathing through his open mouth so the thief would not hear him.

The sounds grew louder. The thief was coming near.

Could Nubians see in the dark? Tom wondered. No, of course not. Their eyes were no different from his. The thief didn't realize where he was going or what lay ahead. In another moment or two, he'd be right next to Tom.

Tom's broad-shouldered build served him well now. He was planted squarely in the middle of the passageway, with his arms stretched out. The thief could not possibly slip by him on either side. Tom had the path blocked.

The footsteps were very close.

Abruptly, Tom sensed that the intruder was only a few feet from him. He lunged, grabbed skinny arms.

"Got you!" Tom yelled. "Don't try to get away!"

The thin, agile figure struggled and squirmed. Tom had the advantages of surprise and greater strength. He locked his arms around his opponent's shoulders, squeezing with all his might.

"Okay," Tom said. "If we can't get out, we'll stay here until the lights go on. But I've got you."

The figure strained against Tom's grip. He was unable to break it. Even if he could not understand Tom's words, he understood that he was a prisoner. If he had to, Tom would hold him for the next hour and a half until Kees showed up to relieve his watch and found that the power had failed. He clasped his hands together more tightly.

Then the captive spoke. In English!

An all-too-familiar, high-pitched voice said, "Do not hold me so tight, Tom. You will make me crush the mask. Let go. I will not run away."

"Ali Hosein?" Tom gasped. "*You?*"

"Ali Hosein, yes. Hello, Tom."

Tom felt sick. His grip faltered and he nearly let go. It was impossible! It couldn't be!

Ali Hosein was the thief!

No, Tom thought. His mind refused to believe it. No! No! No!

CHAPTER FOURTEEN

THE THIEF REVEALED

Slowly Tom let his arms slip to his side. Ali Hosein made no attempt to run away. Tom heard him unwrapping a paper-covered parcel. Then Ali Hosein pushed something bulky into his hands.

"Here it is," Ali Hosein said. "This is what was taken, yes? The mask of gold? Here!"

Tom took it. He ran his fingertips lightly over the cool metal surface. He did not need light to identify the outlines of Akhnaten's strange, long-jawed face. So the mask had been recovered. That was a relief. Yet, to know that Ali Hosein had been the thief—to know that he would have to denounce his cheerful, talkative friend——

"Why did you steal it?" Tom asked. "Why, Ali Hosein?"

"Because I did not want my people to be blamed. I could see how angry you were at us. The yellow-haired man with the cameras called us all thieves. So I took it."

"What are you talking about? You aren't making any sense."

"My English is bad, yes?"

"Your English is fine. It's your ideas that are all scrambled.

167

You stole the mask because you didn't want us to think that you were thieves? What kind of story is that?"

"It is the truth," Ali Hosein said. "I took the mask and came to bring it back here. So it would seem not gone, yes? So it would seem never to have happened? You were asleep. I thought you were. I could go by you into the tunnel, put back the mask——"

"Put *back* the mask!"

"Why else do I bring it with me?"

Tom's jaw dropped. He began to understand at last what Ali Hosein had been doing.

"Tell me, Ali Hosein: where did you find this mask?"

"I find it."

"But where?"

"Oh, it was in village. I find it, bring it back here so everything will be all right again. Yes? We find our way out of here now. The dark—I don't like the dark——"

"Wait a minute," Tom said. "Before we go anywhere, I want to get this story straight. You found the mask—just lying around the village, you say? Where?"

"It does not matter."

"It *does* matter. *Where?*"

"It will only make trouble if I say."

"Tell me, Ali Hosein."

There was a long pause. Then the Nubian boy said, "I did a wrong thing to get it."

"What do you mean?"

"I go into someone's house. I open someone's suitcases. I steal. I am as much a thief as the other one."

"*Suitcases?* Where was the mask, Ali Hosein? I want the

168

whole story. It wasn't a villager who took it out of the tomb, was it?"

"No."

"And it wasn't one of the archaeologists either, was it?"

"No."

"Then it had to be the new people, the tourists," Tom said. "One of them. Is that so, Ali Hosein?"

"Yes. Yes. One of them, he goes into the tunnel, breaks lock, opens gate. Takes the mask. Hides it in a suitcase. Then Dr. Falke gets angry and tells my father that one of our people must have stolen it. I do not want you to think we are thieves. So I get the mask from the thief, I bring it back here. Only that makes me a thief too, you see? That was why I sneak past you. I am a thief who robs another thief. I do wrong like he does wrong."

"No," Tom said. "It's not wrong to undo a theft."

"But I go into his place. I look through his suitcases. This is wrong, very wrong." Ali Hosein laughed nervously. "We go out of here now, yes? Mask is back. All is well. Yes."

"Not just yet. One more thing, first."

"I talk more outside."

"In here, Ali Hosein. Who was the man who stole the mask from the tomb?"

"Must I say?"

"Yes."

"It would make trouble."

"It'll make worse trouble if you don't tell me."

Ali Hosein sighed. "It was the ugly one. With the eyebrows, with the thin face. The guide."

"Paul Kurtz?"

169

"Yes. That is his name. He went into the tunnel while everyone slept. I saw him walking at night. I watched him break lock and go in. Then he comes out, with mask under his arm. Takes it to his sleeping place."

"Why didn't you say anything yesterday about this?"

"I was afraid," Ali Hosein said. "There would be trouble. Loud arguments, name-calling. Simpler this way, I thought. To take the mask from the thief and bring it back here. That way, nobody knows who took it—but mask is back, so it is all right. Now we go?"

"Yes," Tom said. "Now we go. If we can find our way."

He cradled the precious mask carefully in the crook of his arm and stepped forward, Ali Hosein just behind him. It was good to know that Ali Hosein was not actually the thief. The sadness he had felt after catching him red-handed in the tunnel vanished now that he knew that the Nubian boy had taken the mask from the real thief, Paul Kurtz, and was replacing it in the tomb to prevent a fuss.

Or was Ali Hosein the real thief?

Tom realized that it was still possible that Ali Hosein had originally taken the mask from the tomb. Hadn't his eyes glowed at the thought of treasure in the tunnel, right from the start? Suppose he had taken the mask, and then, when the questioning started, had decided to return it to avoid embarrassment. When caught by Tom, he could have invented the whole Kurtz story on the spur of the moment. Ali Hosein was a quick thinker, Tom knew.

Tom didn't want to believe it. But it remained a possibility. Ali Hosein's word alone wasn't enough to prove that Paul Kurtz was the guilty man.

Still, the mask was safe. That was the most important thing, Tom thought.

He shuffled forward into the darkness, reaching with his free hand for the electrical cords.

"Will we get out?" Ali Hosein asked anxiously.

"Sooner or later. When Kees comes on guard duty he'll see that the lights are out, and he'll start the generator again. But maybe we'll find our way before then."

"I hope we do. It is very dark down here. It makes one afraid."

"There's nothing to be afraid of."

"A king is buried here, yes? And if he walks at night? And if we meet him?"

Tom laughed. "You're talking nonsense, Ali Hosein. Akhnaten won't haunt you."

"*Haunt?* What is that word meaning?"

"Never mind," Tom said. "Just stay close behind me and don't worry about anything."

Tom edged forward, his hand grazing the roof of the tunnel. It was beginning to seem as though they would remain lost in the maze of the tomb tunnel until the lights went on. There was no indication of the electrical cords that lined the main tunnel. A chilling thought struck him: what if they were in some endless passageway leading away from the main one? Suppose they got so far from the right path that no one could find them even with the lights on? The maze was fantastically complicated. Underground, shouts for help would be muffled and dulled. It might take weeks for rescuers to explore every byway of the labyrinth—and, without food or water, Tom knew, he and Ali Hosein could last only a few days.

He was debating what to do—whether to keep searching, or to stand still and wait for the main path to be lighted again—when he caught sight of the beam of a flashlight, bouncing off the passage wall not far ahead.

Someone was coming.

But who? Tom nearly yelled out, and only some impulse of caution made him remain silent. He glanced at the luminous dial of his wrist watch and saw that it wasn't yet four o'clock. Kees wasn't due for at least another hour.

He nudged Ali Hosein. "No noise," he whispered.

The flashlight beam was coming closer. It lit the tunnel enough so that Tom could get an idea of the local geography. He saw now that he and Ali Hosein had not been far from the main tunnel at all; they were in a passage that ran at right angles to it, and they were less than ten feet from the crossing of the passages. Tom pushed Ali Hosein back against the wall and flattened himself against it also. The Nubian boy, dimly visible in the faint reflected light, was wide-eyed and bewildered.

A moment later, Tom heard the sound of footsteps. Then he saw a figure come down the main tunnel, step by cautious step, clutching a flashlight and moving slowly forward.

It was Paul Kurtz.

Kurtz went past the mouth of the passage where Tom and Ali Hosein were hiding without noticing them. Tom waited until he had gone about twenty feet down the tunnel. Then he tugged Ali Hosein by the arm, and they began to tiptoe from their hiding place. When he reached the main passage, Tom carefully put the mask of Akhnaten down, so that he would have both hands free. Then he began to follow Kurtz down the tunnel, with Ali Hosein close behind him.

Kurtz was obviously heading for the burial chamber. Tom could imagine what had happened: Kurtz had discovered that the mask was missing from his luggage, and had entered the tomb again to find another treasure to steal. There could be no doubt now that Ali Hosein had told the truth.

Rounding a bend in the tunnel, Tom saw Kurtz just ahead, moving steadily along. He was almost at the burial chamber. Then he reached it. He turned to the right and went in.

Tom waited a few minutes. He wanted to catch Kurtz in the act of robbing the tomb.

Advancing again, Tom crept to the door of Akhnaten's tomb and looked in. Paul Kurtz had propped his flashlight up near the entrance to give him light. He was prowling around a group of alabaster vases near the back of the tomb, evidently hunting for another piece as choice as the golden mask. After a time, he shook his head and turned toward the coffin. His hands reached out to it. Was he going to dare to lift the lid?

Yes, Tom thought. No doubt he hoped to find jewels or golden ornaments within the coffin. No one had lifted that lid in more than thirty centuries. It might hide a pharaoh's glittering treasure.

But no one was supposed to touch that coffin except Dr. Falke's team of archaeologists.

As Kurtz reached for it, Tom stepped into the room and said in a voice so loud he feared the tunnel might cave in from the sound, "What are you doing?"

Kurtz whirled. His jaw sagged and his face turned a horrible fishbelly white as the blood drained from it. He sprang back from the coffin, grabbed one of the heavy alabaster vases, and started to swing it over his head as a weapon.

173

Tom lunged at him.

This was no place for a knockdown battle, Tom knew. The tomb was too small, and contained too many fragile objects. Kurtz had to be put out of commission fast.

Tom caught him around the hips in a football tackle and knocked him sprawling alongside the coffin. The vase flew from Kurtz's hands. Tom winced and waited for the crash, but no crash came. He clung tight to Kurtz. The lean man writhed and struggled. He tried to roll over and push Tom off him, but Tom was heavier, and could hold him down.

Kurtz grew stronger in desperation. His hands shot up and locked round Tom's throat. Tom tugged at them. His face reddened and he fought for breath. He managed to pull the clutching hands away from his windpipe. The feeble light of the flash showed Kurtz's face wild with hatred and rage. Tom gasped, tried to get the man's arms pinned, but Kurtz broke Tom's grip a second time and clawed at his face. Long nails raked Tom's cheek. He grabbed one of Kurtz's wrists, but the other hand came up and went for Tom's throat again.

The man seemed to have a dozen hands. He was fighting frantically, and Tom wondered how long he could hold him.

Then Ali Hosein leaned down and said, "You stop doing trouble or I hit you with this!"

He was holding the alabaster vase. It looked unharmed, and Tom realized he must have caught it when Kurtz let it go. Its blunt, massive end was about six inches above Paul Kurtz's forehead. Kurtz stared upward at it in sudden fear.

"Lie still," Ali Hosein ordered. "Or I knock your brains out, you hear me?"

"All right," Kurtz muttered. "Be careful!"

His body went limp. His hands fell to his sides. Tom relaxed, and warily got to his feet. Ali Hosein still crouched over the man on the floor, ready to crown him with the vase if he moved a muscle.

Tom grinned. "Thanks, Ali Hosein. He almost got loose."

"Just let him move," the Nubian boy said. "I fix him! I fix him good!"

Tom looked around the room. In one corner lay a coil of wire, left over from the installation of the lights. In a few minutes, Kurtz's wrists were tied behind his back. He glowered furiously at Tom as the boys hauled him to his feet.

"Start walking," Tom commanded.

He took the flashlight and prodded Kurtz out of the room. Ali Hosein followed, still carrying the vase.

"Leave that here," Tom said.

"He may do more trouble."

"Not with his hands tied. Put the vase down, Ali Hosein!"

"Oh—all right." The Nubian boy set the vase down carefully.

It was easy to find the way out of the tunnel now. Ali Hosein led, followed by a furious Paul Kurtz. Tom, holding the flashlight, brought up the rear, ready to jump into action if Kurtz tried anything. But the fight had gone out of the man.

When they reached the place where Tom had set down the mask of Akhnaten, they halted and Tom picked up the lovely treasure. He flashed the light on it. For all its adventures in the last few days, the mask seemed unharmed.

"Let's go," Tom said.

Soon they emerged from the mouth of the tunnel. Dawn

was beginning now. The sky was tinged with pink. Tom let his breath out in a long sigh of relief.

"What do we do with him?" Ali Hosein asked.

"We'll take him to Dr. Falke," Tom said. "You go wake your father up. I think he'll want to know that the mask is safe—and that we've got our man."

It was late afternoon. The sun was beginning to sink behind the western hills. The excitement was over. Dave Lloyd sat in front of his hut, crouched over his portable typewriter. Crumpled sheets of yellow paper lay scattered at his feet.

"How does this sound, Tom?" he asked. "Listen:

An archaeological puzzle thirty-three centuries old is about to be answered. The tomb of Akhnaten, the pharaoh who tried to give Egypt a startling new kind of religion, has been found deep in Sudanese Nubia. A team of ten archaeologists from five different nations, working against time as the reservoir of the Aswan High Dam fills, has——"

"You're getting there," Tom said. "But I still don't like it. I think you ought to open with a description of Akhnaten's funeral mask, and then go into all the other stuff."

Dave nodded unhappily. "Maybe you're right. I'll give it another try."

He ripped the sheet from his typewriter and rolled another one in. All afternoon he had been trying to write the lead for his first article about the spectacular new discovery. Dr. Falke had agreed to release the news. When Dave had finished his article, it would be radioed to Cairo and relayed from there to New York. By tomorrow, the world would learn about the most stunning bit of archaeological news since the finding of Tutankhamen's tomb in 1922.

Dave began to clatter away. Tom heard footsteps behind him. Dr. Falke and Sheikh Ibrahim came up, both smiling broadly. The barrel-chested archaeologist clamped a big hand fondly on Tom's shoulder.

"Well, they are gone," Dr. Falke boomed. "The lot of them. I saw the boat steam away."

"What about Kurtz?"

"They will take care of him in Khartoum."

"Will they put him in jail?" Tom asked.

Dr. Falke shook his head. "What good will that do? They are taking away his license as a guide and his visas to enter Egypt and the Sudan. He will never be able to come here again. That is punishment enough."

Tom nodded. Kurtz had confessed his crime that morning. He had run up big debts in his native country. Hearing rumors of an important archaeological discovery, he had hoped to make some money by writing news articles about it.

When Dr. Falke blocked that idea, Kurtz had taken a more direct way of profiting from the discovery. He had slipped into the tunnel to hunt for a salable object, and he had found the golden mask. He knew it would bring a fabulous sum on the black market. But the mask, he said, was stolen from him in turn by one of the natives; he had seen a prowler around the hut where he was staying, and had guessed what had happened. Since he had no way of locating the mask, Kurtz had returned to the tomb to take something else—only to be caught by Tom.

Ali Hosein had admitted his part in the affair too. Sheikh Ibrahim had not been pleased.

"If you knew he had the mask," he told his son angrily, "you should have come to us instead of becoming a thief yourself."

"I didn't want to start trouble," Ali Hosein said. "I only wanted to put the mask back so everyone would be happy."

"You were wrong in what you did," the Sheikh said sternly.

But it was hard to be severe with Ali Hosein. The mask had been found, after all. And Tom knew from the twinkle in Sheikh Ibrahim's eyes that Ali Hosein would not be harshly punished for what he had done.

And now the tourists were gone at last. None of them had been involved in Paul Kurtz's schemes. Kurtz himself was gone, and the golden mask was safe. And Dave had a big story to tell the world.

Dr. Falke said, "Tomorrow we will start to open the coffin. The real work is just beginning for us."

"How long will it take to clear the tomb?" Tom asked.

The archaeologist shook his head. "Who knows? Weeks, maybe months. You know how we work. One thing at a time, and no hurrying. If the coffin is difficult to open, we will have to find ways to do it without harm. The tomb of Tutankhamen kept its finders busy for many years. It may be the same with us, Thomas. We may work until the village is flooded."

"I'll have to leave for home in another month," Tom said. "School will be starting. Is there a chance the coffin will be open by then?"

"Perhaps, and perhaps not. We will see," said Dr. Falke.

"I think it will be a long job, taking many seasons. But you'll return to the Nile, won't you? We'll see you here again, I think."

Tom smiled. Was Dr. Falke a mind reader? Or was it so obvious to everyone that archaeology had Tom in its spell, and that he had made up his mind to come back some day to the land of the pharaohs—not as a sight-seer, but as a full-fledged expedition member?

"I think I'll be back," Tom said. "I'm sure of it, in fact."

"So am I," Dr. Falke said.

Dave continued his staccato typing. Tom walked into the hut and sat down. He had been on the go since three in the morning, and he was as tired now as he had ever been in his life. But the excitement was over. Now began the grueling day-by-day work of investigating the tomb of Akhnaten. At last, the secrets of that dreaming king might be revealed.

A figure stood in the doorway. Ali Hosein.

"Tom?"

"Hello, Ali Hosein."

"I heard you talking to Dr. Falke. Are you going home now?"

"Not for another month," Tom said.

"I am glad. I like you, Tom. Maybe I teach you my language, yes? And we go fishing together. You like fishing?"

"Sure," Tom said. "And I'd like to try to learn your language, too."

"You do me one favor, will you?" Ali Hosein asked. "I ask you now, so I do not forget later."

"Anything," Tom said. "Just name it."

The Nubian boy grinned. "When you go home to America,

you send me something, yes? You mail me a little box of snow, so I can see it. You will do it? Not much snow—only a little."

Tom had trouble holding back his laughter. "All right, Ali Hosein," he said, in a serious tone of voice. "I'll do my best. One box of snow—by air express, special delivery to Nubia!"

AUTHOR'S NOTE

The story you have just read is a mixture of fact and fancy. I think it is important to indicate where the fiction begins and the fact leaves off.

Akhnaten's tomb, at this time, is strictly in the realm of fiction. The rebel pharaoh's body has never been found and most archaeologists believe that it never will be. Most of the experts think that Akhnaten's body was destroyed by the priests of Amon soon after his death. So the central event of the story, the finding of Akhnaten's tomb, is my invention.

However, Akhnaten himself is a genuine figure in Egyptian history. Readers who are interested in learning more about this fascinating ruler may turn to my biography of him, *Akhnaten: The Rebel Pharaoh*. (Philadelphia: Chilton Books, 1964.) Akhnaten's temple in Nubia actually exists, so there is a possibility that his supporters did hide his body in an unknown tomb nearby. Many archaeologists are at work in Nubia today, trying to salvage all the antiquities they can before the waters of the new reservoir make further work impossible. Perhaps the tomb of Akhnaten will indeed be discovered in the next few years, though the chance of this happening is slim.

Several nonfiction books offer more information about the archaeological and geographical background of this story. One of them is mine: *Empires in the Dust* (Philadelphia: Chilton Books, 1963), which tells briefly the story of Egyptology and includes a section on the discovery of Tutankhamen's tomb. A particularly fine book which deals with the effect on Egypt of the Aswan High Dam is Walter A. Fairservis, Jr.'s *The Ancient Kingdoms of the Nile and the Doomed Monuments of Nubia* (New York: Thomas Y. Crowell, 1962.) It has many excellent illustrations of the Nubian ruins. The same author's work, *Egypt, Gift of the Nile* (New York: The Macmillan Co., 1963), is another fine study on Egypt.

A good book on dams in general and the Aswan High Dam in particular is *Rivers in Harness: The Story of Dams*, by Allan H. Cullen (Philadelphia: Chilton Books, 1962). Georg Gerster's article, "Threatened Treasures of the Nile," *National Geographic Magazine*, October 1963, features some striking color photographs of the region that will be affected by the new dam.

—ROBERT SILVERBERG